| DATE DUE | | | |
|---|---|---|---|
| JUL 26 1977 | | APR 1 2 1980 | |
| SEP 17 1977 | | | |
| OCT 11 1977 | | AUG 1 9 '89 | |
| DEC 1 0 1977 | | APR 6 | MAY 2 8 '96 |
| JAN 3 1978 | | JUN 9 '90 | NOV 2 1999 |
| FEB 1 2 | | JUN 2 5 '91 | |
| JUL 2 3 | | | |
| JUN 18 | SEP 11 92 | | |
| MAR 3 1984 | | | |
| APR. 1 1987 | | | |
| SEP 2 4 '87 | | | |
| | | | |

# WEST OF RAILHEAD

# WEST OF RAILHEAD

DWIGHT BENNETT

DOUBLEDAY & COMPANY, INC.

GARDEN CITY, NEW YORK

1977

All of the characters in this book are fictitious,
and any resemblance to actual persons, living or dead,
is purely coincidental.

Library of Congress Cataloging in Publication Data

Bennett, Dwight, 1916–
West of Railhead.

I. Title.
PZ3.N4825We [PS3527.E9178] 813'.5'4
Library of Congress Catalog Card Number 76-55683
ISBN: 0-385-12151-2
✓Copyright © 1977 by Dwight Bennett Newton
All Rights Reserved
Printed in the United States of America
First Edition

# WEST OF RAILHEAD

# CHAPTER I

The river, as it carved its channel over the long tilt of the continent from the Rockies to the Missouri basin, had swung north at one place in a broad curve, like the trajectory of an arrow; it was near the top of this arc that the old crossing lay.

It was a natural ford. For untold centuries buffalo had used it, as had the dark and savage horsemen: Kiowas and Pawnees from the north, Comanches from south of the river boundary that, by long tradition, had divided their hunting grounds. In due time Santa Fe traders with pack trains and canvas-topped wagons had come down to the north bank, making for the distant pueblo huddled about its plaza and drowsing in the sun. And like those others before them, they had descended from the plain to the level river bottom by way of a creek that made easy grade here off the low sandstone bluff.

Until only recently, a clump of cottonwoods spilling along the creek had been used by the Pawnees for ambush against their enemies, both white and red. Now all that was in the past. In this late autumn the trees were stripped, and fallen leaves made a crackling carpet as the rider of the bay sent his horse down the ancient trail on the creek's right bank. Presently the gaunt trees fell back and the river, that men called the Arkansas, spread before him, shining under a flawless sky.

And he drew on the rein, in sudden surprise.

The river flat was perhaps three miles in width at this point, from one low bluff to the other. On the generous and level stretch between him and the crossing, a couple of men were at work. He saw a team and wagon, a tent that looked like old Army surplus. There was a plow, a scatter of supplies, and what looked to be plain trash. A blue feather of smoke rose from a smoldering fire pit, to be tossed and whipped about by the drift of air along the river bottom. The rider had been given no reason to expect any of this, and he took the precaution of opening his coat and making it easier to get at the pistol thrust behind his waist belt. After that he sent the bay forward again.

As he came closer he could see they had been using the plow to run a crisscross of furrows over an area of some half-dozen acres, marking out a kind of grid; now the pair were moving about, pacing distances and pounding stakes and tying colored ribbons to them, and the sounds of their labor carried faintly in this stillness. When one of them caught sight of an approaching horseman he straightened quickly, hammer in hand as he lifted a shading arm against the high sun. He called to his partner and the latter quickly turned. They both stood motionless and watched the stranger emerge from the background of leafless cottonwoods.

He was a spare figure in the saddle, well and neatly dressed despite the dust that had settled on him. He could have been forty or a little less, clean-shaven, his face not darkly tanned beneath the brim of a flat-crowned planter's hat. His nose had a slightly hawkish line to it, his eyes were cool and observing and almost the color of the pale blue stone in the ring on his left hand. He drew rein beside the man with the hammer, looked from him to the other one who came walking briskly toward them now across the flat and plow-furrowed ground.

"So, what's all this about?" he said dryly.

The one with the hammer, in bib overalls and a faded hickory shirt, said belligerently with a twang of Missouri in his voice, "What's it look like? We're marking out a townsite."

"That's rather what I thought," the other said, looking down from his saddle on the busy results of their labor. "Well, there's new metropolises springing up like weeds, all over the prairie. I suppose some of them will even make it."

"You can lay your bets on this one," the second man told him, having arrived in time to hear his comment. "Just look at the location." He was carrying a flattened stake, and he turned to point with it across the wide valley, toward the silent sliding of the glassy water lying adazzle under the sun. "This river bottom's the only feasible route once the railroad starts building again out of Newton. From Hutchinson west, there'll be no grading problems all the way to the Colorado line. We hear a lot of speculation as to which route they'll actually take, but by our figuring there's no question. They *have* to follow the river."

"You've a reasonable argument," the horseman conceded. "And another advantage you may not have considered: the old traders' road to Santa Fe that I've just ridden down from Ellsworth." He indicated the creek trail, breaking off the shallow rim. "Commerce follows the natural routes. It's no accident this was where the trail joined the river—so, I admit you've happened on a good natural spot for your town, on more than one count."

The two town builders nodded in satisfaction, on hearing that. The one in overalls had the definite look of a farmer, with drab, untrimmed hair and rather porcine features that had been burned brick red by years of fierce exposure to the elements. His partner was smaller and thinner, narrow of face, with red-tinged hair and a foxy aggressiveness and the shrewd glance of a small town businessman. He showed a gold tooth as he smiled briefly. "It's clear enough," he told the stranger, "you're a man that knows how to use his eyes. We've got coffee brewing," he added, indicating the fire ring, "and stew and biscuits in the dutch oven. We were just about to knock off for dinner. Will you join us?"

The rider looked at the noon position of the sun and appeared to decide it might be as well to accept. He dismounted—a little stiffly, as though not accustomed to long hours in the saddle; having eased the saddle girth and slipped the bit so his animal could crop the autumn-cured grass, he walked over to the wagon where his hosts were dishing up grub into tin plates and pouring coffee. An ancient-looking rifle, its stock reinforced with a wrapping of baling wire, leaned against one of the spoked wheels; the stranger took it in with a casual glance, as he accepted plate and cup and eating utensils from the one in overalls.

"Nat Colby's the name," the man told him. "This here's my cousin, Virgil Beason—we're from Neosho, over across the Missouri line." He didn't appear to notice that the other made no move to identify himself. "If you're interested," he went on without pause, "you got a real chance to get in on the ground floor here. Plenty of choice building sites still available."

Actually not one SOLD marker had, as yet, been erected to mar the unbroken expanse of staked-out lots. If the stranger was aware of this, he made no comment. He placed his steaming coffee cup on the wagon tailgate, preferring to eat standing after his hours of riding, and worked at the stew while he listened silently to Nat Colby's sales pitch.

After a moment he asked, "Do you have a name yet for this town you're planning?"

"It ain't definite." The man shot an uneasy glance in his partner's direction, as though to see if he were listening; this seemed to be a thing of some dispute. "Seein' as I'm the one staked the pre-emption, I kind of favor 'Colbyville.' What would *you* think of that?"

Dry amusement touched the stranger's lips. "Not an awful lot. I'd say 'Colbyville' sounds like the back end of nowhere. You need a name that paints pictures—one to act on the imagination."

"Yeah?" The brick-red face was scowling. "Like for instance?"

The other looked around, seeking his answer in some landmark on the flat and featureless stretch of river bottom. His glance touched upon the low bluff, the tongue of gaunt cottonwoods that spilled down the creek to pool their leafless branches at the southeast corner of the townsite.

"Well, what's wrong with 'Paradise—'" He corrected himself. "No, '*Eden* Grove?' Now, doesn't that suggest the place a man might like to put down his roots, and raise himself a family?"

"Eden Grove . . ." The red-faced man repeated the name slowly, testing the sound of it; but his scowl remained and the stranger shrugged again, dismissing the whole matter.

Virgil Beason, he of the sharp glance and the narrow features, came over swirling coffee in a cup. He took a drink, spat out the grounds between prominent teeth. "You told us you came down from Ellsworth," he said abruptly and, as the stranger nodded: "I hear they did right well this year, with the Texas cattle trade."

"True enough—they shipped a fair number of head out of their stock pens. Of course, it was only their first full season; they should manage even better in seventy-two."

"*We* might have something to say about that!" Beason assured him complacently. "This town of ours will put Ellsworth and Abilene and Newton and those other places clean out of business. One thing, we're forty miles closer to Texas—and every day you cut off a drive that length has got to make a difference.

"Even more important, we're west of the Texas quarantine line.

Those towns farther east act like the line don't even exist; but it's there—right on the statute books. One of these days the farmers and such are going to raise enough fuss, the state of Kansas will have to do something about enforcing it so as to keep out the tick fever they say the longhorns bring north with them. And when *that* happens, the only shipping pens not closed to Texas cattle will be the ones right here—on the flats of the Arkansas River!"

He made a sweeping gesture, so eloquent one could believe he already envisioned the stockyards and the gleaming rails, heard the bawling of cattle and the shouting of trail crews shoving them aboard the waiting cars. No question about it, this Virgil Beason seemed to have some of the true promoter's gift for making another see the things he imagined—almost, to see streets and buildings and people where now was only barren earth.

But if the stranger felt this, he neglected to show it. He turned and placed his empty plate and cup on the wagon tailgate. "Well," he said, "I thank you for the hospitality. I'll have to be getting on—a considerable ride ahead of me."

"Heading south . . ." murmured Beason thoughtfully. "For Texas, maybe? Would you be having an interest in the cattle trade, yourself?"

The other's mouth quirked in a half smile, as though he found something amusing in that. "Indirectly, I suppose you could say so."

He didn't explain his cryptic answer, and Beason didn't press him, saying instead, "You might pass the word, then. By next season we'll be in business—or even if we aren't, because the railroad for some reason might not have built this far, it can still be a handy stopover on a direct route to the Ellsworth market. Tell your friends about us."

The stranger didn't commit himself with more than the briefest of nods. He turned away to his horse that grazed nearby. He replaced the bit, pulled up on the cinch strap, and swung into the leather. After that he returned to the wagon where the cousins were still finishing their leisurely meal. He paused a moment to look down at them from the saddle.

"One thing strikes me," he said. "I see no evidence this property of yours has ever been surveyed."

Nat Colby lifted a meaty shoulder within his sweated farmer's shirt. "Why pay some damn fancy pants with a tripod, when any fool can pace it out using a few stakes and maybe a ball of string?"

"You miss the point. The law requires that it be surveyed— Didn't you know that?" He saw his answer in the blank puzzlement of the man's face. "Maybe you haven't really looked into the Townsite Act. Besides a surveyor, for your town to be legally platted, you also need the services of a probate judge. Then there's the filing fees; and along with that, you have to be ready to lay out the full purchase price of your land—in advance."

The cousins were staring at him. Virgil Beason said roughly, "We never heard anything of all this!"

"You never asked, then!" the stranger retorted. "They do say ignorance is bliss. Apparently you two had some idea you could pull yourselves up by your own bootstraps—stake free land and make your fortunes selling town lots without having paid out a dime from your own pockets. Well, I'm afraid it doesn't work that way. Establishing a townsite can run into money." He cast a cool glance over the poverty-stricken outfit scattered about the river flats. "And it doesn't look to me there's too much of that around here."

Colby found a strangled voice, somewhere inside his thick chest; his sweating face was contorted with emotion. "What you saying all this for?" he cried, almost incoherent. "You tryin' to tell us we've only been wasting our time? Damn you, it ain't true! It's nothing but lies!"

The stranger seemed more amused than offended. "Suit yourselves," he said. "Here's one more thing for you to think about, supposing the railroad does run its right-of-way up the valley: What if it turns out you've gone and filed on a railroad section? That would mean you could end up having to pay for your land twice over!" And leaving them stunned with that thought, he touched a finger to hatbrim—the blue stone of the ring flashing pale fire— and turned his horse.

Behind him, as he started on toward the shallow river crossing, Nat Colby all at once broke free from where he stood rooted. "Damn you!" he cried. *"Damn you!* Come back here!" Suddenly, like one demented, he flung himself at the wagon, snatched up the ancient rifle, and ran stumbling after the horseman. And when the latter neither halted nor looked around, Colby set himself and whipped the rifle to his shoulder, with trembling hands, and fired.

The shot kicked the weapon's muzzle high, a film of smoke springing from it; the weapon's roar ran booming along the flat. For a moment, that seemed the only result. The bay horse continued moving at an easy walk toward the sliding water, then abruptly it halted, tossing its head to pull at the reins. Slowly the rider bowed his head, slowly he folded at the middle, and went spilling out of the saddle in a loose and boneless fall.

As Nat Colby stared, his cousin came hurrying and snatched the smoking rifle from his hands. "What the hell was that for?" Beason demanded harshly.

The other turned, his features slack with shock. "You heard him!" he cried hoarsely. "He was making fun of us! He was trying to tell us we couldn't—couldn't—" Suddenly, at the collapse of his dream, the man's face broke in bitter disappointment and tears flowed, unchecked, through the stubble on his cheeks.

Virgil Beason swore, long and furiously. "Nat Colby," he said, "you are a damned fool if you *are* my kin! I always knew it; but—*this!*" He looked again at the body sprawled motionless where the horse had dumped it from the saddle, and now he walked forward to see at closer hand the result of his cousin's bullet. The latter followed, stumbling a little over the uneven ground, still shaking in the aftermath of what he had done.

The bay had quickly got over any uneasiness and fallen to pulling again at the grass. The stranger lay on his back—hat fallen from his head, face turned to the sky. He looked rather thoroughly dead. But now, as the two approached with dry grass whipping about their legs, the limp body moved. The head turned and the eyes settled on Beason, in the lead. And the right hand made a jerking move toward the gun that they could see, now, shoved behind his waistband.

In a single motion, Virgil Beason brought up the muzzle of the rifle, levered in a shell, and fired.

The frightened horse gave a squeal as it shied. At such close range, this second bullet slammed the downed man hard, making all his limbs jerk convulsively. And then he went completely still. Staring down at him, Beason justified himself to his companion:

"Well, you saw him. He was still alive and reaching for his gun. I had no choice but to finish the fool thing you started."

After that neither spoke during a long moment, while they stared at the dead man. Nat Colby stood rubbing sweating palms up and down the front of his overalls. "What—what are we going to do with him?" he demanded hoarsely.

The other shrugged. "Take him and plant him somewhere, of course—and then forget we ever saw him!" He frowned. "I wonder who in the world he was?"

"Way he's fixed out," Colby conjectured shakily, "he coulda been one of them big-shot Texas cattle dealers, heading home after cleaning up at the Ellsworth market. Could maybe have some money on him. . . ."

"I wonder. . . ."

Suddenly Virgil Beason was down on one knee, laying the smoking rifle aside. He seemed to feel no compunction against touching the body in spite of the blood from the shattering drive of the bullet. He ran his hands over the man's clothing, searching for a wallet.

At something he found, he paused. Abruptly he tore open the bloody shirt, revealing a canvas belt strapped about the waist, next to the hide. He located the fastenings, fumbled with them, and with an effort pulled the belt free, the body giving limply. Metal clinked. His own fingers beginning to shake, Virgil Beason ripped open one of the pouches, and another.

He looked up at his cousin. His hands were filled with the glint of coins, the green of folded paper.

# CHAPTER II

To Clark Tanner, following this wagon road west along the right-of-way from Hutchinson seemed like traveling backward in time, in order to view the construction of a railroad in reverse. During the first fifteen miles or so, work trains passed them hauling materials up to end of track; there, on the second day out, they found the steel gang muscling bright new rails into position and spiking them down. After this scene was left behind, the plodding team and creaking wheels carried him and Parley Newcome on past miles of leveled roadbed, with ties spaced and waiting for the rails, until presently they caught up with a crew that was laying down the heavy balks, from stacks that filled the July afternoon with a strong odor of creosote.

Here Clark Tanner halted his team and, with a newspaperman's penchant for asking questions, shared a drink with the straw boss and a chat concerning the progress of the job—how many miles of track were being laid each week, what unexpected problems might be rising, and so on. But the foreman might have caught some touch of the professional behind his questions, or perhaps he recognized the bulky shape of the hand press under lashed-down tarpaulin in the back of the wagon; at any rate he became cautious with his answers and soon gruffly excused himself. Tanner shrugged and climbed back to the wagon's seat, his left hip paining him as he settled there beside Parley Newcome. They tooled ahead, high weeds between the tire ruts whipping at the axles and the sun an eye-punishing dazzle in the pale summer sky.

They were well past the region of track and tie laying, now. For a distance the graders had been at work, preparing and leveling the right-of-way; soon that too fell back and then there was nothing to be seen, except for some intermittent surveyors' stakes, to indicate that a railroad was being built along the river bottom.

Newcome had a dry observation. "The way that fellow talked, you'd think they was really killing themselves. All I can say is, they should have seen the work Grenville Dodge got out of his crews when he was pushing the U.P. across Wyoming, three-four years back. I've seen days when they put down five miles of completed track between sunup and dark. And once they even made it ten!" Newcome had been there; he had been nearly everywhere, apparently, in thirty years of following the printer's trade—at least Clark Tanner had never caught him telling a story that didn't hold the ring of fact.

He was a dried-up little man, the graying hair lying close to his round skull in thinning patches, blue eyes faded, and shoulders rounded from years of laboring over a hand press and sorting type from the hellbox. Every crease and wrinkle of his hands was too deeply etched in printer's ink for him ever to get them clean. And he bore that other stigma of his rootless breed—the rather crippling and pathetic dependency on alcohol that seemed part of the makeup of every tramp printer, rendering him unable to hold a steady job for any length of time. He had been with Tanner for over a year—a near record with him, apparently. In a print shop, there was nothing at all he couldn't handle.

Clark Tanner said, "There's no comparing this operation with the pressure Dodge had to work under."

"You can say that again! Way those loafers back there are poking along, don't look to me they'll ever get out of Kansas."

"They'll have to by New Year's, or from what I hear they stand to lose their land grants." Tanner meant the government's subsidy of alternate sections, on either side of the right-of-way, donated free and clear to encourage construction of new rail lines across public domain. "So you can count on it—somebody is going to start pouring the heat to them pretty soon now."

Newcome shrugged stooped shoulders. "With more than two hundred miles of steel to lay down, they damned well better!"

The fourth evening west of Hutchinson, nearly at the end of their journey, there was some question in Tanner's mind which would give out first—the long summer twilight, or the crowbait wagon horses. Finally, as an explosion of sunset faded and sky and river both turned to steel, he turned his rig into a clump of scrub where they would have something to make a fire.

He refused his helper's offer to take care of the team, and while Parley Newcome set about preparing their supper, he unharnessed and watered the animals and hobbled them on the rank grass; they needed grain, but he had none at all for them. Limping because his lame hip hurt him severely after these many hours on the hard wagon seat, he proceeded to check his bulky load, making sure the dead weight under the tarpaulin hadn't shifted. The left rear wheel bothered him; it was developing a bad wobble, and when he gave it a kick the dry spokes rattled.

He knew he should take the wheel off and soak it in the river overnight, but that would involve unloading the wagon and he didn't feel up to the effort. Presumably there were only a few more miles to go and he was fairly sure the old rig would hold together that long.

The prairie night closed down as cicadas buzzed and the river murmured within its banks. Curtains of heated air, rising from the earth that had stored it through the long day, caused the stars to flicker. The two men ate their meal in silence, each thinking soberly of tomorrow; soon after, for the last time, they bedded down beneath their wagon.

With daylight Parley Newcome's hands were shaking badly; but this was no unusual thing and he knew the remedy—several long drags at the bottle he kept under the wagon seat, and then the minutes of humiliation and shame while he waited for the whiskey that he depended on, as on a crutch, to have its effect. Clark Tanner always pretended not to notice this ritual, but the other man understood he wasn't fooled. Afterward, with the fiery burn of alcohol taking hold in his empty belly, Newcome fell quietly to his share of the morning's chores.

When the horses had been taken to water and coffee put on to boil, Clark Tanner got his razor and soap and a pan of heated water. Newcome, who only scraped the stubble off his own wrinkled cheeks when he happened to think about it, respected his boss's careful attention to the matter of shaving. Not that there was any vanity in Clark Tanner; he was simply a young man of average height and fairly homely appearance, who felt he ought to try and look his best. Slicing bacon into a fry pan, Parley Newcome watched him and was aware that the other man's hands, too, were trembling as they worked the razor over his rather gaunted cheeks; but with Tanner, it was not the whiskey shakes.

"How you feeling?" the older man asked, on impulse.

The black eyes, that looked back at him from the mirror propped upon a wagon wheel, were noncommittal. "Good enough."

"Oh, sure. . . ." Newcome shrugged, knowing his boss was lying.

You could tell by the way he moved. On a good day, in spite of that hip smashed by Morg DuShane's bullet, he could usually get around in a way that made the limp hardly noticeable. This morning he was having trouble. Even Newcome, who could sleep anywhere at all, knew that the hard ground and nothing more than a blanket to soften it must have given Clark Tanner a bad night.

Because of Tanner's patience and unbending charity toward another man's problems and weaknesses, Parley Newcome would have laid down his life for this boss of his—but what could you do with a man who never complained and who would not let himself accept sympathy?

They ate without much talk. The day brightened rapidly; by the time they had cleaned up and the gear was stowed away and the team once more in its battered harness, the sun was a smear in the eastern sky, pouring its heat upon the land. Neither man seemed to have anything to say, as the wagon rolled out upon this last leg of the journey. Perhaps neither would have wanted the other to sense his own uncertainty, with the end of the trail drawing close.

It came with early noon. The first they saw was the flickering leaves of cottonwoods growing along a muddy creek—the tallest trees they'd come across in miles of following the river bottom. Where this creek met the twin ruts of the wagon track, someone had constructed a plank bridge of unpainted timbers, so new they still gleamed faintly yellow. Just beyond, lay the town itself.

The wagon rumbled off the bridge and climbed the farther bank, and in tree shade Clark Tanner pulled in his team.

A banner, strung across the street between a couple of poles, bore in ornate lettering the message: WELCOME TO EDEN GROVE— FASTEST GROWING CITY IN THE WEST. Parley Newcome looked at it and then again at the trees above their heads, the leaves shaking and barely filtering the smash of sunlight. "I suppose that's the Grove," he said dryly. "Fancy name, for a spindly bunch of cottonwoods. And calling this a city is pretty fancy, too!"

Some dozen scattered buildings in various stages of completion faced the line of railway stakes, three or four to the block and straggling away along the north side of the wagon track which, at this point, could probably be called a street. They all appeared to be business houses, with wooden false fronts; signboards on the few that were completed identified two or three saloons, a restaurant, a couple of mercantile establishments; down at the far end, Tanner saw a high-peaked roof he thought might belong to a livery stable. The largest building, the hotel, actually boasted a second story and glistened with a coat of whitewash—the only one in town, that he could see.

Behind this single line of buildings, and its sheds and privies, another half dozen were scattered as though at random across the townsite. Only one or two looked like residences; for the time being, Tanner supposed the men who owned places of business were probably living in them. He did see a few weather-stained tents, pitched among the stacks of lumber, and the wood scraps and trash covering the vacant lots. Sounds of saw and hammer ran thinly through the noon quiet; somewhere a rooster crowed.

Such was the city of Eden Grove on a summer noontime in this year of 1872.

Clark Tanner could not have said what he expected; if he was disappointed he would not admit it, to himself or to the other man beside him. Instead he pointed to the smear of high sunlight on a web of yellow timbers lying south of the unfinished right-of-way, between it and the riverbank. "You'll notice," he said, "they're already putting up their loading pens. Someone has that much confidence of getting a share of the Texas cattle trade, once the railroad reaches here."

"Apparently you go along with that."

"Well, the town is better situated than Ellsworth or Abilene or Wichita: It's closer to Texas and west of the more settled sections of Kansas. Yes, I can't help thinking it has a real chance," Clark Tanner said.

"I used to be an optimist myself," Parley Newcome admitted,

"but I've had most of that knocked out of me. Still I hope you're right." He added, "And unless I'm mistaken, we're looking at a bunch of people who are hoping the same thing."

Tanner understood what he meant. From their place on the wagon seat, they could watch the flow of life in this single, sketchy main street of Eden Grove. There wasn't any wheeled traffic, except for a canvas-topped dray that was backed up at a loading dock and discharging freight for one of the stores. There were men, however—a stream of them, flowing along the weedy path that was only here and there interrupted by a stretch of wooden sidewalk.

None of them seemed to have any particular business. They passed in and out of the saloons, and collected in knots under the shadow of wooden awnings. Tanner couldn't begin to count them, but he thought there must be close to a hundred. He noticed no women, at all.

He had seen farmers in rural areas, during times of drought, collect on village street corners to squint at the sun-blasted sky and debate the chances of rain. He was somehow reminded of that in these men's behavior, though they didn't look at all like farmers. They wore town clothes of one sort or another. Watching their gestures as they talked, Clark Tanner said dryly, "My guess is, they're all waiting for someone to make them rich."

"Damned boomers!" the other agreed, sourly. "I seen plenty of the kind in them towns along the U.P.—always hungry for a chance to make something for nothing. And most of them only ending up hungrier."

"And drifting on to the next place, as soon as that one petered out." Tanner's mouth quirked at the irony of a thought that struck him. "Maybe they're not really all that different from *me!*"

That got him a look, and a protest. "Oh, come on now! Be fair! You had some tough luck. You may be on the move but no one would call you a drifter."

"No?" Tanner lifted a shoulder within the threadbare coat. "So what else *would* you say? Unless maybe that I'm hunting a game to buy into, with damn few chips that are worth anything: just what I managed to get out of Nebraska with—a hand press and a few fonts of type."

Parley Newcome looked a little grim as he added, "And an

ounce of lead from Morgan DuShane's pistol! It was blind, dumb
luck that he only managed to put that bullet in your leg, instead
of your gut. . . . And what thanks did you ever get for trying to
whip the corruption in that damn town?"

"I keep telling you, what happened a year ago in Nebraska is
past and done. Maybe, at least, it taught me a lesson or two about
minding my own business!"

The old man wagged his grizzled head. "Sorry to hear you talk
like that—*I'm* supposed to be the cynic in this outfit. But I can't
help but wonder," he added, and took a further dubious look at
the few raw, unpainted buildings, the empty streets and lots with
their littering of trash, the aimless milling of purposeless men.
"Now that you've seen it, are you sure as you were that this town
is what you want? Could you for instance consider spending your
life here?"

"I haven't seen all of it," Tanner pointed out gruffly. "And it
hasn't seen me." He lifted the reins. "Might as well take a good
look, after the distance we traveled to get here."

Under the sting of rein ends against bony rumps, the team reluctantly drew the wagon forward, up the last grade from creek
level and out from under the shifting shade of the cottonwoods.

Buffeted by hot Kansas wind, the overhead banner billowed and
tugged at its lanyards and popped with a sound that became, as
they approached this first intersection, almost as loud as the reports of a pistol. On the near corner stood a building whose sign
identified it as the headquarters of the Eden Grove Townsite
Company and Railroad Land Office—N. Colby & V. Beason,
Props. Tanner said, "Yonder looks like as good a place as any to
ask a few questions."

He halted his team beside a dusty stretch of dry grass and
weeds, where grasshoppers snapped and whirred about the wagon's wheels. He anchored the reins to the brake handle. "What
do you want me to be doing?" Newcome demanded.

"You could take the horses down to that creek and water them.
Afterwards it might be an idea if you were to stay pretty much in
sight of the wagon. Somebody might take a notion to start nosing
around."

"Yeah." Nothing had to be said about staying out of the town's
saloons—Clark Tanner knew, whatever his faults, the older man

could be trusted to keep his drinking separate from his duty to a
job. Leaving him in charge, Tanner climbed awkwardly down,
favoring that hurt leg as best he could. He started for the land
office.

A clot of idlers had taken refuge under its wooden awning,
where they stood in the shade chewing and spitting and trading
rumors as to when the railroad might be expected to reach here.
Two weeks, Tanner heard one say; and then there was a storm of
debate, as each man shortened or lengthened the time according
to whatever rumor he favored. On the day the first train did roll
in, though, all seemed agreed the population of Eden Grove
would triple overnight—and, with it, the value of every town lot
and nearby acre of farmland.

Tanner left them counting their future wealth and limped inside the building through its propped-open double doors.

It was dark in there, after the blast of sunlight, and not noticea-
bly cooler. The room was sparsely furnished; beyond a divider railing he saw a couple of desks, a wooden file cabinet, a tall safe in
one corner with a painting of a sailing ship on its door. At one of
the desks a man with the appearance of a clerk was copying en-
tries into a ledger, while utterly ignoring a group of boomers simi-
lar to the ones outside; these were clustered before a large map
nailed to a wall strut, and Tanner went over for a look past their
shoulders.

It was a map of the townsite. The cottonwoods were there, and
the creek, running down the map's eastern edge. He saw "Railroad Avenue" and above that "Federal" and then "Union"; while
the cross streets, beginning at this lower right-hand corner of A
Street and Railroad Avenue where the townsite office stood, were
named for the letters of the alphabet. Crosshatchings in pen and
ink would indicate that a good many lots, within an area of some
four blocks square based on the railroad right-of-way, had already
been sold; the rest of the plat, he noticed, was still mostly blank.

Tanner left the boomers pawing it in their endless speculation
and went over to the railing. After he had waited patiently for
some minutes the clerk finally had to acknowledge his presence,
rising as he laid down his pen.

He created an instinctive dislike in Clark Tanner. He was a
supercilious young man, coolly impervious to the heat in a high

collar and a waistcoat, his shining black hair slicked tight and parted in the middle. He gave a look to the other's dusty clothing and said, in a tone of considerable doubt, "Can I be of assistance?"

"I don't know. Are you the boss here?"

"I'm in charge of the office," the clerk answered stiffly. "I also have full authority act for Mr. Beason and Mr. Colby when they don't happen to be present."

"That's all right," Clark Tanner said. "I imagine they're the ones I'd want to see. When will they be in?"

"Mr. Colby stepped out for an hour or so," the clerk told him. "Mr. Beason is on business in Hutchinson, but I expect him back today." He was looking at the stranger with closer attention; perhaps, in the latter's remarks, he detected a possible customer. "If you're interested in property, there's really no need to wait. I can show you some very attractive business or residential lots. Or, if you want to know about farm acreage, we are authorized agents for the railroad lands in this section of Kansas."

"The town is built on railroad land?"

"No, no. The original townsite is part of a government preemption claim filed by Mr. Nat Colby. The railroad owns the right-of-way, of course, and a section to the south adjoining it; but we've acquired title to as much of that as we intend incorporating in the city limits.

"If you'd care to step over here, and let me show you on the official plat—"

Tanner shook his head. "Not now. Maybe I'll look in again, later on."

The clerk shrugged his indifference and turned away; but by now Tanner had caught the attention of the boomers and he could feel their stares following him as he made his way outside again. He turned along the street to see more of the town for himself, the sun striking him as he stepped from beneath the land company's wooden awning. But a hand dropped upon his shoulder and he looked about sharply, to see a man who had been studying the map and who had apparently trailed him from the office.

This man grinned at him and said, "You were smart, friend. It's a den of thieves in there. Beason, and Colby—they're set on milking this townsite for every dime they can squeeze out of it!"

When the other merely looked at him he drew nearer to explain, in friendly confidence, "Prices that are being asked for a stinking little old town lot, with nothing but a patch of prickly pear on it—it's just ridiculous! I've only been here a week, and far as I'm concerned it's already gone out of sight. Anyway, I have other interests that need looking after back in Kansas City, and so I'm leaving here tomorrow. I got no choice."

Guessing what was coming, and coldly amused, Clark Tanner waited for it as the man continued: "There's a little problem, though. Happens I've got something here"—and he brought the folded paper from his pocket—"a real honey of a lot, over on Union betwixt C and D Streets. I hate to, but to close a quick deal I'm ready to take a loss on it. Friend, I'll even let you open by naming a price. . . ."

"Thanks all the same," Tanner shut him off. "But, no—really. I wouldn't want to take advantage of you." He left the man standing there openmouthed, the deed in his hand.

Three times within the next two blocks Clark Tanner found himself being stopped by men only too eager to offer him a bargain in lots, whose deeds they just happened to own but could be made to part with. He gave them all short shrift. He supposed these rootless boomers would stand around, swapping lies and rumors and selling property to each other and drinking up their paper profits in the town's barrooms, right up to the moment when the railroad finally arrived. But not one of them would have had anything to do with whether the town actually lived or died.

Eden Grove, if it grew and prospered, would owe it to the ones who were backing their vision by putting up buildings and establishing businesses here on Railroad Avenue. Tanner stopped in the doorway of the New York Restaurant, finding it barely large enough for a counter and stools and a couple of square tables. The bald-headed proprietor had a full house of drifters and speculators keeping him busy at the moment, and Tanner passed on. More promising was the hardware and furniture store in the next block, where a heavy freight wagon was still disgorging a load of crates onto the raised front stoop; a man wearing alpaca sleeve protectors checked them against a bill of lading, while workmen finished emptying the rig and toting the heavy boxes inside. Here, at least, was a man who plainly expected to see his business grow, and Clark Tanner put him down as one worth talking to later when the man was free.

That left him two more blocks to cover—a half-dozen buildings, mostly jimcrack wooden shanties with the gaps of vacant lots between. So far what he had seen was not particularly encouraging, but his sights were set on the gleaming, white-painted hotel. Until he had been there, at least, he meant to withhold final judgment.

C Street, like B and A, had been marked out crudely with a couple of furrows of the plow, but so far hadn't seen enough traffic to beat down the rank grass and actually turn it into a thoroughfare. Tanner crossed, passing a corner saloon whose open door exuded a fair share of whiskey smells and loud boomer talk. Only one other building on this block had been completed, its signboard identifying it as a grocery and general mercantile. Clark Tanner had already decided he would turn in here, before he got a look at the occupants of a farm wagon that had drawn up in front.

They had the appearance of a homesteader's family, probably in off their quarter section for supplies, or to do other business. The rig and team looked serviceable but not in much better shape than the ones that had brought Clark Tanner here. The woman on the seat, and the three youngsters in the back, were clean and neatly dressed but in clothing that had lost most of its original color, leached out by constant washings and by the fierce prairie sun.

The children were towheads in various sizes; when he smiled and winked at the little girl she ducked shyly out of view behind the side of the wagon box. But it was the woman who somehow hit him hard, as he saw the look she gave him between the wings of her faded sunbonnet. The eyes in the plain, sunburned face seemed wary, frightened, like those of a trapped animal ready to bolt. The work-roughened hands in her lap were knotted defensively. Tanner recognized extreme timidity; he knew how it could be sometimes for one of these frontier women—isolated from the world in the bleak loneliness of a prairie soddy, no one in miles except for her own family.

This one was not really old—something other than time had gaunted the woman down and bowed her shoulders. He'd seen her type before, too—in Nebraska. A mover's wife, he thought, probably dragged from farm to farm, and from failure to failure, while long despair had its way with her.

And now she was here; and as he turned up the steps into the store, taking the image of her haunted face with him, he reflected that for some, at least, this Eden Grove was proving to be no paradise. . . .

# CHAPTER III

The mercantile was, at least, open and ready for business. The store boasted a fair stock of supplies, considering its newness and that of the town it served. There were shelves of airtights, bins of onions and potatoes, barrels of flour and crackers and molasses, and a big jar of pickles on the counter. And there was room for other things: tin basins, bags of feed and grain, stacks of cheap clothing and straw hats and a row of kerosene lamps gleaming on a shelf. In fact, if he looked hard enough, Tanner thought, a customer could probably locate nearly anything he needed.

He was well inside the door before it occurred to him he might have walked in on a quarrel.

One of the three people in the room had to be the father of the brood in the wagon—he had the same yellow hair, the color of new rope, and it contrasted oddly with the weathering of his craggy German features. His neck was like a pillar, set on thick shoulders rounded by toil. There was a boy with him, older than his brothers and sister waiting outside; though he had almost a man's full growth, Tanner judged him for perhaps fifteen. Like his father he wore overalls, but his feet were bare.

The farmer was speaking, as Tanner entered, in a voice that held heavy traces of German accent. "Ma'am," he told the woman behind the counter, "I already tell you I don't argue this with no woman. I know it's none of your doing. I want I should talk to Sam Harolday."

"My husband is out," she answered. "You just saw me go and look."

"Yes ma'am. But I still think he's here—much as I don't like I should call anyone a liar. Now, you go back and say Emil Burkhalter's waiting, and I don't leave till I see him."

The woman, Clark Tanner thought, could have been a beauty.

There was a certain delicate modeling to her cheeks beneath the wide-set eyes, a high rounding of the brow set off by the darkly golden hair massed above it, a mouth that was made for smiling. But the gold seemed to have faded, and bitterness or disappointment had done things to the smile and to the candor of her glance. Just now she was angry. Her head lifted and she said tightly, "If you question my word—"

But he was already looking past her, to a curtained doorway at the rear of the room and to the man who had suddenly appeared there. In his shirt sleeves, a grocer's apron tied about his slim middle, the newcomer said sharply, "All right, Burkhalter. Is something the matter?"

The big German retorted, "I think something's the matter, when a man makes his wife tell lies for him! I got good ears, Mr. Harolday. I hear you back there just now, telling her you don't want to see me."

"Nonsense!" Harolday snapped, but Tanner guessed the high color in the storekeeper's face came as much from embarrassment at being caught as it did from anger. He was a man of considerable dignity—he looked more like a banker than a storekeeper, Clark Tanner would have said; the apron tied about his waist seemed out of place. He was slim and fairly tall, with chiseled features and full sideburns whose black was just frosting to gray. He seemed a man whose pride could be easily stung, and this hulking farmer had just done it.

But he tried to brush the whole matter aside, saying impatiently, "I'm a busy man. What's so important that Mrs. Harolday couldn't have tended to it?"

"I think you know that too," Emil Burkhalter said. "I already tell your missus once, and you heard me. I want to know about interest."

"What about it, then?"

"I hear feller say you charge me interest on the things I take from store. Is true?"

"Of course," the other said. "It's customary with open accounts. But you were informed of that."

"Was not! Mr. Beason only say, 'Anything you need to get started on your land, you tell Sam Harolday your credit is good at store.' That is all. Nobody say about interest!"

"You're mistaken," Harolday corrected him coldly. "I told you myself, that first day you came in. Apparently you forgot."

Watching unnoticed, Clark Tanner wondered how far Burkhalter meant to carry this argument. But perhaps, with his German training, he felt overawed by the storekeeper's certainty and by the authority he represented. The stiffness went out of the thick shoulders; the work-tough hands, that had been knotted into fists, loosened. When he spoke again it was to demand sullenly, "So how much you charge me?"

"The same as all our customers," the other man told him. "Nothing for thirty days, then eight per cent a month on the balance."

"*Eight* per cent!"

"If that seems high," Sam Harolday pointed out coolly, "stop and think a moment of the risk involved in extending credit, where there's practically no way to enforce collection. Beason and Colby have to protect themselves."

The farmer's head jerked up. "You saying I don't pay?"

"Not you personally, of course. But the ones who don't, unfortunately, make it necessary to put an extra burden on the rest who are honest. I know it's not fair, but it's always been that way and always will be." He added crisply, "Now, I'm very busy. If you've come in for more supplies, just give the order to Mrs. Harolday, and she'll be glad to take care of it for you and add it to your bill."

But the other man was not to be put off. "No! First, I want I should see how much you say I owe now. I want to see figures."

"Very well." The storekeeper looked at his wife, who turned and went through the curtained doorway into the rear of the building. She was back again almost at once, before Clark Tanner had time to tell himself he was watching a private scene that was none of his business and that he really ought to withdraw. The woman had a thick ledger which she handed to her husband; Harolday laid it on the counter, leafed through it until he found what he was looking for. Turning the book, then, he stabbed a finger at the open page. "There you are," he said curtly. "Look for yourself."

Emil Burkhalter picked up the book, held it for better light. He stared at the figures a moment, and then his head lifted and angry speech tumbled from him. "Robbers!" His voice was suddenly hoarse with outrage. "How long you think it take me to pay *this*? After buying quarter section, you know I got no money left. Before I can raise cash crop—or enough even my family don't go hungry—I'll be so far in debt to you thieves, I never get out already!"

Harolday's face had gone white. "If you can't discuss your business calmly—"

"By damn!" the other roared. "I show you calmly!" And he hurled the heavy ledger straight at the storekeeper.

It took Harolday squarely in the chest. It was surprise, probably, more than the book's weight that staggered him. Tanner didn't know whether the man simply lost his head, then, or actually thought the other was coming over the counter after him; but Harolday swore fiercely and made a lunge toward a shelf beneath the counter. He came up with a long-barreled Colt revolver in his hand.

What alarmed Clark Tanner was that the big German obviously had no weapon at all; it struck him that Sam Harolday might be about to commit murder before the very eyes of his wife. The thought was enough to drag a horrified outcry from Tanner; but Emil Burkhalter had seen the gun, and he acted with speed that might not have been expected from one who appeared that big and clumsy. He took a single, solid step forward and, reaching, caught the wrist that held the gun and clamped it down, hard, upon the counter top. Harolday cursed him and tried to break free, and they struggled briefly.

The gun went off, a thunderous sound trapped within the four walls. The woman screamed.

Exploding powder built a balloon of black smoke that surrounded the struggling men; it shifted enough to show that the bullet had apparently done no damage. But the shot had jarred Tanner loose from where he stood and it brought him hastily forward, not sure what he meant to do. And as usual when he wanted to hurry, that damnable crippled leg held him back.

The German had balled one craggy fist. With Harolday's arm and the smoking revolver pinned down, Burkhalter began clubbing him in the face. At the second blow a smear of blood sprang out on the storekeeper's cheek; by then Tanner had managed to reach them and he grabbed the bigger man's arm. Burkhalter gave him the briefest of looks and, almost negligently, swung the arm to dislodge him. Even so, except for the bad leg Tanner might have hung on; but he lost balance and was shaken loose and sent stumbling against one of the bins of vegetables.

He took the blow squarely on that injured hip. He heard the cry of pain that was torn from him, as the leg gave way and let him slide helplessly down to hands and knees. There was one moment of searing agony. After that his head cleared and with it his vision.

The scuffle between the German and the storekeeper appeared to have ended as abruptly as it began. A hand lay on Tanner's shoulder; he looked up to see someone leaning over him, mild brown eyes peering anxiously through steel-rimmed spectacles. The face was seamed and hollow-cheeked, the brown mustache shot with gray. The face said, "Are you hurt?"

"No," he answered hoarsely. "I'm all right."

To prove it, he grabbed the edge of the bin and pulled himself to his feet, but he could hardly conceal a momentary stagger or the tightening of his facial muscles. The other man had straightened with him; he was not tall—hardly average height, and his clothing carried a mingled odor of tobacco and another, medicinal smell that was explained as he said, "Look—I'm a doctor. I think perhaps—"

But Tanner doggedly shook his head. "It's all right. I'm stuck with a bum hip and I just have to be careful with it."

Drawn by the shot, undoubtedly, and the woman's scream and the noise of scuffling, a number of other newcomers had entered the store; they nearly filled it. At one side Emil Burkhalter stood glowering sullenly, with his tall, towheaded youngster beside him and, also, the woman from the wagon; they both seemed ready to defend him with their lives or, perhaps, to hold him back from committing further violence. Meanwhile, behind the counter, the storekeeper had whipped off his apron and was dabbing at his cheek with it, frowning as he saw the stain of blood. And he was eyeing, with wary caution, another man who had just stooped and picked up a smoking pistol from the floor.

"Who does this belong to?"

"It's mine," Harolday answered curtly. "I keep it here under the counter, for protection."

"I see. . . ." The man turned and looked thoughtfully at the big German—probably, Clark Tanner guessed, pondering the thought of Harolday's need of a gun to protect himself against someone who was clearly unarmed.

The man looked to be in his late thirties, with thinning blond hair and a quiet manner and a cool gray eye that seemed to put considerable weight on the one he looked at. Harolday appeared to feel something in it that bothered him. He flushed and said sharply, "Damn it, Phil, the man attacked me! He came in making all kinds of wild charges, and—"

"All right, Sam," the other said, holding up a hand. "That's between the two of you. Apparently nobody's too bad hurt—but, it's a wonder someone wasn't killed."

Though no one had asked him, Clark Tanner felt impelled to put in a word. "I saw what happened," he told them. "The shot was an accident. I don't think he had any real intention of using the gun."

They all looked at him. If Sam Harolday was pleased at the unexpected word of support, he didn't say anything. The one who held the gun also considered the stranger a moment; then he shrugged and, turning, laid the weapon on the counter. "I would just suggest, Sam," he commented dryly, "that you had better be a little more careful in the future."

"Then this man," Harolday retorted, glaring at the big German, "had better watch his tongue!"

The farmer lifted a massive fist, stabbing a blunt forefinger at the man behind the counter. "I got nothing more to say to you," he declared loudly, "except that Emil Burkhalter never yet refused to pay an honest debt. My family should starve first! But I also tell you, never again I buy another thing in *this* store!"

"Suit yourself!"

Burkhalter was already turning away; with both big hands spread to move his wife and son ahead of him toward the door like someone shooing chickens. And on their going, this brief excitement ended, and the curious who had collected to see it began to break up and drift away again; the store gradually emptied.

The gray-eyed man was observing the storekeeper with a dry interest. "Interest rates again, was it, Sam?" he suggested. "You really ought to tell that pair you work for, they're getting a bad name that could end up hurting their business."

When the other merely looked at him, not answering, he turned to Harolday's wife who had had nothing at all to say during this. "Afternoon, Lucy," he said, and turned to go.

The doctor meanwhile had been observing Sam Harolday with a professional's eye; now he said, "How about letting me fix that cheek for you?"

"No," the storekeeper said gruffly. "He just skinned it a little."

And with that he left them, disappearing through the curtained doorway. The doctor watched him go, with a shrug. "If nobody wants my services, there's no reason for me to stay." To Clark Tanner he added, "The name's John Riggs. I have an office on Federal. Anytime you might want to drop in, I'll be glad to look at that hip."

"Nothing to look at, Doc," he answered briefly. "I got sort of smashed up, a year ago, and this is the way it healed. It's just a matter of getting used to it."

Riggs nodded his shaggy head, in sympathy. Then the gray-eyed man approached them and he added, "This is Phil Steadman. You saw the hotel, of course—biggest building in town? It's his."

Returning the other's nod, Tanner gave his own name. "I'm a newspaperman," he said, and saw the quick interest in both his hearers. "I understand Eden Grove doesn't have a paper yet. I came here with the idea of starting one. Brought my press and equipment with me."

"Good enough!" Steadman told him. "Now we can finally begin to *sound* like a town. Count on me for an ad in every issue."

"Why, thanks. I only just got here," he added. "I've been looking around, getting the feel of the place."

"And walked in on a brawl! Well, I suppose there's no quicker way. . . ."

The doctor said, "If you've got questions, Phil's the man to answer them. He's been on the townsite almost from the beginning." And Steadman suggested, "Why don't we all go along to the hotel—have a drink and something to eat and talk things over?"

Tanner hesitated only briefly, thinking that Parley Newcome

had been left quite a while now with the wagon and might be wondering what had become of him. But Newcome could shift for himself, and this was too good an opportunity to learn some needed information, however biased it might be. So he said, "That sounds fine," and accordingly the three men left the grocery together.

As they stepped out onto the rough wooden stoop, the wagon with Emil Burkhalter seated beside his wife, and his brood in the wagon bed behind him, went creeping slowly away along the single line of buildings that was Railroad Avenue. Looking after them, Clark Tanner wondered where the big German would turn, now, to get the things he needed for his poverty-stricken family.

The store having emptied, Lucy Harolday turned back through the inner doorway and into the living quarters at the rear. This, one day, was planned to be a stock room, with one section partitioned into an office for her husband; but such plans had to wait until a time when he could afford to build them a house. For now, the family was making do here as best they could.

It was crowded enough, everything crammed into one room—a bed in one corner, a crib for the baby, a wood stove and cooking area, a sink and a table and few other furnishings. Jeanie was seated on the bed, playing quietly and wholly absorbed with her doll; angry voices—even the report of a gunshot—hadn't been enough to disturb her placid and contented nature. Lucy paused to lay a hand upon the small head, on the fine, fair hair that was so much like her own. She went on, then, to the table where her husband had filled a basin with warm water from the stove and was gingerly dabbing at his cheek with a dampened cloth. The water in the basin was faintly tinged with red.

She made no offer to help. She asked coolly, "Does it hurt?"

"What do you think?" His reply was angry and petulant. "Of course it hurts. The damned krauthead!"

"You shouldn't have threatened him with a gun."

Sam Harolday could scarcely have missed the lack of sympathy in his wife's tone. He looked at her as he retorted, "Was I supposed to stand there and let him assault me? Those fists of his . . . I could have been disfigured!"

"Yes, that *would* have been a calamity."

"Meaning, you wouldn't even have cared!"

They looked at each other across the gulf of a failed marriage. Sam Harolday was clearly primed for another of what had become a series of increasingly bitter quarrels, but suddenly his wife felt a weariness so great that she could not find the energy to flare back at him.

When she didn't answer he prodded her. "It's the truth, isn't it?"

She took a slow breath, that lifted her breasts within the prim shirtwaist. She said, in a tone that held little life, "There was a time I'd have cared terribly—when I was the proudest woman I knew, being married to the handsomest man in the county. How long ago was it, Sam? How many miles from here?"

But she didn't want a quarrel in front of the child; she turned away to busy herself with something at the stove. Sam Harolday, though, was not willing to let the matter drop. Without looking at him, as he followed her across the room, she could almost see the scowling look on his deceptively handsome face.

"I try to understand you," he exclaimed. "I try to be patient. I know you hate this town—I know you resent me bringing you here. But can't *you* try to have a little patience? Won't you at least give me, and the town, a chance? After all my rotten run of luck, I should think you'd have sympathy enough not to begrudge me this second chance."

*Second chance?* she thought. *Or third—or fourth?* How many did he want, this Sam Harolday, with his clean good looks and manner that seemed to suggest every solid quality, but was actually no more than a façade for weakness, and indecision, and poor judgment; this husband of hers, who had failed so many times and now was reduced to managing a store for men they both knew to be petty scoundrels, in a town that was not yet even a town. . . .

When she did not answer him, his voice took on self-righteous resentment. "I just hope you took a good look at that woman who was in the store just now—Emil Burkhalter's wife! Think of her, and then ask yourself what reason *you* have to complain. Even at the worst of times, have you ever lacked for anything? Have I let you go hungry, or cold? I suppose you've worked your hands to the bone, like *that* poor woman?"

Lucy Harolday was barely able to believe her ears—that a man with all his advantages should boast of having done better than some poor immigrant dirt farmer! It swung her around to face him; but then she could only nod and say, in a dead voice, "Yes, Sam. You've given me everything except the one thing I needed most— a reason to be proud of you!"

They neither one pursued the matter further.

# CHAPTER IV

The hotel, just beyond the juncture of Railroad Avenue and D Street, had a corner entrance and a gallery across the front. With its whitewash the noon sun fairly made it dazzle—summer's heat and the dust-laden prairie wind were still to do their work of blistering and scouring. As he accompanied Phil Steadman up the three broad steps to the veranda, Tanner clenched his jaws in the effort not to let that injured hip betray him; but even so, he had an idea that the doctor, bringing up the rear, was reading him correctly. He probably couldn't fool John Riggs's practiced professional eye.

Steadman, though, certainly appeared unaware. He was interested only in showing off his hotel, in which he obviously took great pride. So Tanner hobbled dutifully after as he led the way into the lobby, with its Spartan furnishings. The desk, near the stairs, was presided over by a solemn young man of twenty or so whom Steadman introduced as his nephew. Through a square archway Tanner was shown into the dining room—boomers crowding a couple of trestle tables and bouncing their voices off the walls, steaming bowls and platters of food being passed and emptied and refilled again by a stout black woman who appeared to combine the jobs of waitress and cook.

Steadman even wanted his guest to see the kitchen. Tanner trailed him out there and duly admired the gleaming black stove and the spotless equipment, though the aromas that assailed him made his jaws ache and set his empty belly rumbling. Back to the lobby then, and Tanner was eyeing the stairs in some apprehension and wondering how long his leg would hold out when to his relief the hotelkeeper said, "I wish I could show you the rooms, but I'm full up just now with these boomers—in some cases three and four to a bed. Others come here without a dime in their pockets and sleep out in the brush, and yet they all seem to think they're going to make a fortune."

Frowning, Clark Tanner said, "With such a mob hanging around and nothing to keep them out of mischief, I'd think the town would have a real problem keeping order."

"You're damned right it's a problem! Since we're not incorporated yet, it means there's no actual law closer than the nearest county seat. Maybe you noticed the way Doc and I came running today, the minute we heard a gunshot? That's the reason."

Tanner admitted dryly, "I noticed."

"So far, with it all we've been lucky—no gunplay; a few drunks, a few fights that we've managed to break up before they turned destructive or anyone was bad hurt. Still, it's a powder keg and we know it."

"I'm afraid you'll really know it, if things work out and the cattle trade finds its way here. If a man can judge from the stories out of Ellsworth and Abilene."

Steadman nodded soberly. "That's something that will have to be faced when it comes. Being where we are, west of the Texas fever quarantine line, there's not a doubt in my mind the cattle trade is coming to Eden Grove sooner or later. And we know what will surely follow it: the gambling and the saloons and the women."

"So doesn't it look as though you ought to be pushing for incorporation as quick as possible? It would help, to have a city government and an adequate police force in place ahead of time."

Tanner heard a sound from Doc Riggs, that he took to be a grunt of agreement. But Phil Steadman hesitated. "There are problems with that," he answered, a little vaguely. Almost as though he wanted to change the subject he added, "Let me show you the bar. . . ."

Through a second door, adjoining the lobby, it was fairly small but serviceable—a low-ceilinged room with a plain wooden counter, no mirror or fancy glass behind it, no crystal chandelier. There wasn't the noisy crowd of quarreling boomers here that Tanner had noticed in the town's saloons. Steadman found an empty table near a window, where they could look past the gallery railing to the bronze smear of sunlight on the river; Clark Tanner swallowed a groan of relief as he slid himself into a chair, able at last to ease the pain of his hip.

Having signaled the bartender for a bottle and glasses, Phil Steadman said, "We could all use something to eat, couldn't we? I'll go arrange it." And he left Tanner and the doctor seated at the table, with the warm wind through the open window bringing the smells of dust and heated lumber and, behind these, the dark odors of the river.

During all this, Riggs had let the others do the talking, never opening his mouth. Now, as he uncorked and poured drinks for them both, he looked at Tanner through his spectacles and said, "So you're a newspaperman?"

"It's what I like to call myself." He was glad for the drink, but he took it down slowly, not wanting to give the impression of needing it. Still, he was aware of the doctor studying him across the rim of his own glass, and he could guess at the speculations running through the older man's head—trying to put the crippled leg and the other pieces of the picture together.

"Any particular reason you picked a place like this to set up in business?" Riggs added quickly, "I suppose you could ask me the same question. I guess I haven't any good answer except that there are people here, and they have their right to a doctor when they need one. And I don't see any other candidates."

"I suppose my reasons are pretty much the same," Tanner admitted. "A man starting out has to make a choice between trying to buck an established paper, or going someplace that's too new to have one yet. And so, I'm here."

"Any family?" the doctor wanted to know, and when he shook his head, "Nor have I. That makes our choices easier."

Riggs picked up the bottle, offering with a gesture to refill Tanner's glass; the latter quickly indicated he'd had enough. "Speaking of families," he said as the other poured himself another small shot, "can you tell me anything about that fellow Burkhalter, who had trouble at the store?"

"What do you want to know? Emil Burkhalter is a hard-working man, but I'd call him an unlucky one. In the past, I gather he's worked here and there as hired help; his wife, too. He's tried renting; finally, from somewhere, he seems to have scraped together enough for his quarter section, a couple miles north and west of town.

"For all I hear, he's having a tough time of it out there; but who doesn't, trying to scratch a farm from this Kansas hardpan? Too, there's been some illness: the wife and the little girl. I have to charge him *something* for looking after them. He's got that stubborn German pride—he wouldn't take charity."

"I heard him say he'd run out of money, and no crop yet. How long can he hope to make it without credit of any sort?"

"I don't know. I really don't." Riggs emptied his glass and made a face over it. In an abrupt change of subject he asked, "You have your press with you?" And as the other nodded: "Where are you setting up?"

Tanner admitted, "That's something I've got to arrange. I haven't any ideas yet."

"I might have one. There happens to be an empty building next to mine, around the corner on Federal. Plenty of space, living quarters in the back. The man who built it was a topnotch carpenter and cabinetmaker; he did a lot of the work on this hotel. He intended opening a shop, but he died suddenly—heart attack. I couldn't do a thing. And his wife had no choice but to sell the property back to the townsite company and go home to her people in Illinois, I think. Anyway, the building's sitting there, waiting for a new owner."

"Sounds interesting," Clark Tanner agreed. "Worth looking into. The townsite company—that's these two men, Beason and Colby?"

The doctor nodded. "Yes, those are who you'd be dealing with." He was frowning as he said it; he seemed to hesitate before he added, more slowly, "Maybe it's none of my business, but I feel I should tell you—" He was interrupted by the return of Phil Steadman, followed by his nephew; the latter carried a tray with plates of food, and the hotel owner had a steaming coffee pot.

As these were being set out on the table, a man detached himself from the group at the bar and came over, a drink in his hand. He was not one of the boomers—Steadman introduced him as Tom McDougall, the owner of the livery stable, and waved him into the extra chair. He was cadaverously lean, with a prominent nose and a black beard he wore chopped short an inch below his chin. His clothing gave off a faint odor of straw and grain and horse manure, but Clark Tanner was too busy eating to let it bother him.

"I've been in a number of businesses," Steadman was saying as he ate, punctuating his remarks with gestures of knife and fork, "in a good number of different places. Right now I have faith in this Eden Grove. I think the town is going to last; if I didn't, I wouldn't put so much into it. I don't mind confessing I'm borrowed up pretty heavily, investing in this hotel."

Sawing at a piece of beefsteak, Doc Riggs said dryly, "I trust you didn't do your borrowing from Colby and Beason."

For some reason that got a thin smile from the hotelkeeper and an emphatic shake of the head. "My connections are in Kansas City."

Clark Tanner spoke up. "Colby and Beason: I've heard almost no other names since I got here. Aside from the fact that they founded the town and own the townsite company and the store that Sam Harolday manages for them—what else should I know about them?"

He had a sudden feeling that no one at the table was in a hurry to speak, each waiting for someone else. Finally, with a faint shrug of his shoulders within the coat he wore in spite of the day's muggy heat, Riggs put his coffee cup down and said, "I suppose you'd have to call them controversial. Nat Colby was a Missouri dirt farmer, and now that he has money he still thinks and talks like one; but that cousin of his bears watching. He plays his cards close to his vest, and any dealings you have with him you'll do well to be careful."

McDougall's head had lifted sharply. Now the liveryman broke in: "I have to challenge that! Virg Beason is simply a smart man. He has to be, to hold his own against all the grifters who have come flocking in here, ready to grab off everything in sight. Colby's nothing—as dumb as they make 'em; you could steal *him* blind three times a week. But Virg has brains enough for the two of them."

"His methods are too cold-blooded for me," John Riggs insisted. "I'd hate to be the one he gets his hooks into."

"All right, so he does a shrewd business. That's how he stays on top! All I got to say to people like you, Doc, is that except for

Virg Beason, there'd be no town here at all. Who is it that's getting stockyards built—and has agents in the field down in Texas right now, working to bring us the cattle business that will put Eden Grove on the map?"

"And who is it," the doctor reminded him, in his mild voice, "that's standing in the way of incorporation, which is the one thing this town needs most—and I mean *now*, before those Texans get here and bring us real trouble?"

"Ahhh!" With a sound of disgust, McDougall slapped the table with both palms, causing silverware to chime in the dishes, and pushed up to his feet. His black eyes sparked anger. "John," he said, "you're a pretty fair hand at setting a broken bone, and for the most part I have to respect your judgment. But there's too much jealous talk being made. I thought you knew better than to add your voice to it."

John Riggs seemed to consider a rejoinder, but in the end he passed it off and returned to his eating. Not getting an answer, Tom McDougall made an impatient slicing gesture and strode out of the bar. In the silence he left behind, the doctor sawed off a piece of meat and put it in his mouth. Chewing, he glanced aside at Clark Tanner. "I told you the subject was controversial."

"Yes, you see how it is," Phil Steadman added, frowning. "You'll hear it both ways, depending on who you talk to about Virgil Beason. He's that kind of man—everyone has his own opinion."

"Then I suppose I'll just have to wait and form my own."

"You shouldn't have to wait long," the doctor remarked, and pointed with his fork at the window. "That's him, handling the horses."

Tanner bent his head a little to get a clear look past the gallery railing. A two-seated rig, dusty with travel, was just heading west past the hotel. Four men and their baggage were crowded onto the double seats; he had only a glimpse of the erect, spare figure holding the reins, as Riggs continued, "I have to give it to the man—he never lets up! He has more push and energy than I have, by a long way. Apparently he's just got in from Hutchinson; he's back there every time he can, meeting the trains and beating the drums for Eden Grove, and fetching prospects out with him."

"Three this time," the hotel man commented. "As usual he'll

take them for a look at the stockyards, and then he'll bring them here. Gives me maybe ten minutes to figure where I'm going to cram them in! Excuse me," and pushing back his half-empty plate he rose and hurriedly left them. The rig and team had gone on out of sight, leaving a faint stain of dust in the air beyond the veranda railing. Tanner and the doctor returned to their meal.

Ten minutes later, having finished, they entered the lobby and found Phil Steadman already greeting the three latest arrivals from railhead at Hutchinson.

They looked like businessmen, several cuts above the usual run of boomer—seemingly, Virgil Beason had a good eye for sorting out prospects. Now, as Steadman invited his new guests to register at the desk, Riggs gave Tanner a nod and led him over to the one they had earlier seen driving the surrey. "Beason," he said, without preliminary, "here's a fellow you should talk to. Clark Tanner's the name. He thinks he might be interested in that property next to mine—the Whitney building."

Virgil Beason turned his head, and Tanner looked into a pair of the most coldly calculating eyes he thought he had ever met up with. "The truth of the matter is," he explained, "I've got a newspaper office—and no place as yet to put it."

"A newspaper?" The shrewd, fox-sharp features showed a kindling of interest; the mouth shaped itself into a smile, and Tanner saw the glint of a gold tooth. "That's interesting. Have you looked at the building, Mr. Tanner?"

"Not yet. I haven't been in town but an hour or so. The doctor here was telling me about it."

Apparently satisfied that those other men could be left for now with the hotel man, Beason said, "It's only a block over. I've got my rig. Why don't we just swing around there?"

"Fair enough."

To the doctor Beason added, "Give you a lift, John?"

But the latter shook his head and said briefly, "No thanks," his voice without warmth. Clark Tanner had a feeling that John Riggs chose to be under no obligation to Virgil Beason, even for a ride around the corner. He stood fingering a pipe he'd taken from his coat pocket, watching without expression as the other two left him and headed for the surrey and team waiting at the veranda steps.

By contrast with Railroad Avenue, there had been no great amount of construction yet on Federal—only four completed buildings that Tanner could see, along its entire length; north of this the townsite lay nearly vacant. In the yard behind a one-storied clapboard shack, someone's washing, snapping and fluttering in the warm wind, made a spot of dazzling brightness.

The empty carpenter's shop stood north of the hotel, a weedy alleyway between. When the surrey halted, Tanner managed the long step to the ground and joined Virgil Beason, as the latter sorted through a ring of keys and found one to open the padlock holding the stout door closed. The building had been shut up for weeks; the dead air, when they entered, was heavy with the smell of sun-heated lumber. Beason stood back to let Tanner make his inspection.

There was no question that the building would be perfectly suited. It was solidly constructed, with plenty of windows, and entrances front and rear. In the living quarters at the back he noticed a wood stove that had been left behind. Tanner walked about, planning how he could use the space—the hand press to go here, the composing table and banks of type yonder, a desk and files near the west window. . . .

Virgil Beason said finally, with a trace of impatience, "Well? Appears to me you could hardly do better for what you want. I can make you a good price."

Tanner hesitated before he asked, "Would you consider renting?"

He'd had a strong suspicion Beason was not going to take to the idea. "Renting? That's something I hadn't considered. I'm afraid I'd have to think it over."

"I'll be honest," Tanner said bluntly. "I've got my equipment, and a fair amount of print stock—I'd be prepared to put out the first weekly issue inside a few days. What I'm short of at the moment is cash. Still, I should be able to manage a month's rent if the terms were agreeable. Otherwise—" He let the sentence die.

Beason was clearly displeased. But after a long surveyal that seemed to probe deep and take the other's measure, he answered, "You realize I have a partner that would have to be consulted. Why don't we go down to the office and talk it over?"

"All right," Clark Tanner said. And so the padlock was snapped in place, and Virgil Beason turned his rig and they made their way again through the raw, half-formed town—between the still unpainted buildings and the staked and empty lots, the piles of raw lumber and the occasional tent whose canvas snapped and tugged in the hot wind. As they passed one of the saloons, idlers in the doorway recognized the promoter of Eden Grove and hailed him; Beason acknowledged the greeting with a brief nod.

When they drew up before the townsite office, Tanner checked to make sure his team and wagon, with its bulky cargo under tarpaulin, still stood where he had left them; no sign at the moment of Parley Newcome, but Tanner knew his helper would be somewhere close, keeping an eye on things.

The office was empty except for a man Tanner hadn't seen before who was seated at a desk, scowling over something he was busily writing. This, he supposed, must be the other partner. Nothing at all had changed since his earlier visit; it was the talk he had been hearing about the pair that gave Tanner an uncomfortable feeling—with Nat Colby lifting his head to stare at him, and Virgil Beason entering just behind—that this was almost like walking into a den of wolves.

# CHAPTER V

Once again Clark Tanner heard himself being introduced as a newspaperman, come to offer Eden Grove a service it badly needed; this time, however, the reaction was different. Having heard his partner out, Nat Colby continued to stare at the stranger with a look that could only be described as dark suspicion. He made no offer to shake hands.

Tanner remembered hearing him called a Missouri dirt farmer; seeing him there hunched behind his desk—the sunburned face, the work-gnarled hand that engulfed the pen he had been writing with—it was easy to believe. Colby was in his shirt sleeves, but his cravat and flowered waistcoat and heavy-linked gold watch chain looked as though they had cost money, and they looked out of place on him. So, especially, did the ring on his thick finger—Clark Tanner pegged it as almost surely a genuine sapphire.

Tanner was a little puzzled. He'd hardly have supposed a half-sold townsite would have paid off quite so well, or quite this soon; but it did appear this Nat Colby was enjoying what must be the first financial windfall of his life.

Leaning against the railing that divided the office, arms folded and one leg crossed over the other, Virgil Beason continued with his explanation. "First order of business is finding Mr. Tanner somewhere to put out his paper. We were just now looking at the Whitney building. He's suggested he might rent it from us."

"Oh?" Colby's scowling stare switched to his partner. "I don't go for that. Hell! Ain't there enough details now to drive us crazy, without getting mixed up with trying to collect rent?"

"That was my own first reaction," his cousin agreed. "But there's other towns that would likely welcome this man if we let him get away from us. And we damn well need a paper."

"Why?"

Beason shrugged. "If you can't see that, there's not much chance of my explaining it to you." He showed Tanner a faint smile. "I'm afraid my cousin never had proper schooling. He lacks respect for the printed word."

"Now, hold on there!" Colby's head jerked, red-burned face darkening. But his partner ignored him.

"Mr. Tanner," he said, "you've looked over our city; you've met some of our people. You see how far we've come in the six months since my cousin's original pre-emption claim was staked. And it can only be a matter of weeks before the railroad finally gets here, and things really start to boom.

"But obviously we wouldn't even be talking if you weren't already convinced Eden Grove is a city with a future. To show you *my* confidence, I'll make a proposition: I'll personally subsidize your paper. You can have the building rent free for three months, and in addition I'll meet any reasonable expenses for the same length of time. How does that sound?"

"Don't I get no say in this?" Nat Colby broke in indignantly. Beason cut him off with a shake of the head.

"This is my affair. You made it plain you weren't interested. . . . Well, Tanner? What do you say?"

He couldn't answer at once. Generosity was the last thing he would have expected from Virgil Beason; he found himself probing the suggestion, looking for danger. "You hardly know me," he objected. "You haven't even seen my equipment. You don't know if I'm qualified to run a paper."

"All right. So I'm gambling a little." One shoulder lifted in a shrug. "I'm used to making judgments about men; I think you'll do. As for the paper itself, there needn't be any problem. All I ask is to see the copy for each issue before it goes to press."

Tanner looked at him. "You mean, you want editorial approval?" he said carefully.

"I suppose that's what you call it."

He should have expected as much, Clark Tanner thought. He tried to hide his disappointment, and to ignore the narrowing of the man's eyes as he said, "Sorry, but I can't allow that. If I did, it wouldn't be my paper. So, I guess we can't make a deal. Thanks for your time, anyway."

Already headed for the door, he was halted by Beason's voice speaking behind him. "One question, Tanner. How would you see the policy of this paper of yours?"

Slowly turning, he tried to read the other's face as he worded his answer. "Why, to tell the facts as I see them," he answered briefly. "And promote the future of Eden Grove."

Those shrewd, corrupt eyes seemed to bore into him, to dig at the thought behind the words. And then, abruptly, Virgil Beason nodded and his whole manner changed. "I can't see what more anyone could ask than that." He came toward the other man then, offering his hand. "All right, friend. No one wants to run your paper for you. It'll be strictly hands off—and my offer still stands. How about it?"

Some deep suspicion, working within Clark Tanner, told him there was still time to say *no*. He had to believe that there was no good in trusting this man. . . . But then he thought of the long and bitter road that had brought him to this town, and this moment. He thought of his empty pockets and the ancient wagon that might not last the distance, hauling him and his press to some other town.

He drew a breath and made his decision. "Sounds worth a try," he said, and took the proffered hand—it felt muscular and dry. "I might as well hunt up my printer and get my stuff moved in."

Beason showed him one of his brief smiles, with the glint of a gold tooth in it somewhere. "Good enough," he said and added casually, as the other turned to go, "Oh, and you can tell Sam Harolday, at the store—any supplies you need, I said to give you all the credit you want."

For the briefest moment, Tanner stiffened. But Virgil Beason's smile was bland enough, betraying no hint of a trap; Clark Tanner kept his voice level as he answered carefully, "Thanks." A moment later he was gone.

Looking after him, Nat Colby told his cousin, "I hope the hell you know what you're doing!"

The other made an impatient gesture. "If you weren't so stupid, you'd realize a new town like this has Goddamn well *got* to have a newspaper in order to hold its own. I've been trying for months to get us one—and now we have it dropped right in our laps."

"Well, just don't forget—the whole thing was your idea, and none of mine."

"I'm not likely to forget it," Beason said dryly. He went through the opening in the railing, picked up a letter from his desk and glanced at it; he tossed it down again and looked at his cousin who was still glowering and muttering under his breath. "Will you come out with it?" he demanded. "What gravels you about this?"

Colby's chair creaked under him as he swung around to say angrily, "I suppose you've forgotten that story they printed about us, in the Wichita paper? I spent a solid hour talking to that reporter—and then he made me out some kind of a damned hayseed!"

"So that's it!" Beason shook his head. "Can't you see, that's exactly what I'm getting at? They're *scared* of us in Wichita. They know we're going to take business away from them; naturally they're out to make us look as bad as possible. We got to be able to hit back."

"But how do you know where you are, with this fellow Tanner? He stood there and told you, to your face, he don't mean to give us any say in what he prints. I don't trust no newspaper feller," Nat Colby said stubbornly. "He could be out to trick us—just like that bastard from Wichita."

"Didn't you *look* at him?" his cousin exclaimed, exasperated. "Believe me! He might talk big, but anyone with half an eye can see he's flat broke; and on top of that he's a cripple. If he ever had any fight, something's taken it out of him."

A sound of creaking wheels and rattling timbers brought their eyes to the open door, as an ancient wagon lumbered past. Clark Tanner held the reins, with a second man on the seat beyond him. They could see the miscellaneous shape of the freight in the wagon box, lashed down under canvas. Virgil Beason nodded as the rig crawled on out of sight.

"That's one sorry outfit! Give such a man three months' free rent, and all his expenses paid, and he'll be tamed. He won't bite the hand that feeds him—he'll be too busy licking it."

"And if you happen to be wrong?" his cousin suggested gruffly. "If he wants to give us trouble?"

Beason shrugged. "Then we simply get rid of him—and end up with his newspaper. Take my word for it, there's no way we can lose. . . ."

Unloading everything from the old wagon was a long job and took what was left of the afternoon. What had been salvaged from the fiasco in Nebraska, a year ago, was little enough—hardly anything really, aside from the bare essentials of print-shop equipment—but it was all heavy and bulky and made a tough job for two men. Worst of all was the ancient hand press, an awkward and outsized dead weight. It was the last item to come out of the wagon; by the time they were able to maneuver it to the ground and then through the too-narrow door into the building, both men were exhausted.

Clark Tanner's injured hip felt like searing coals, while Parley Newcome's hands were trembling so badly he could scarcely control them. His boss pretended not to notice when he returned to the wagon and spent several minutes doing something by the front wheel; by the time Newcome re-entered the building his cheeks were flushed, but he had regained his steadiness.

The stuff from the wagon had been strewn more or less haphazardly about the big room, with the hand press that had given them so much trouble dominating the clutter; final work of separating and placing things in some kind of order could wait until tomorrow. Tanner had built a fire in the stove and broken out enough of their dwindling supplies to put together a meal. As they ate beans and bacon from tin plates, seated on packing cases, he explained his hopes for the immediate future.

"What we have to do is try to get out the first week's edition as quick as possible, and then start drumming up ads and subscriptions. I've got one ad promised, for a start—Steadman, at the hotel. Meanwhile, I was thinking, there's the wagon and team—they aren't much but I might be able to turn something on them at the livery, to help keep us going."

"But I thought you had a deal with this Beason gent," Newcome said, frowning. "I thought he was underwriting your first three months."

Tanner's mouth was grim. "I don't want to be under obligation to Virgil Beason, and I think it's exactly where he'd like to have me. He told me my credit was good at that store he owns—but he said nothing about the eight per cent a month his manager charges on open accounts."

Parley Newcome stared. He gave a low whistle. "Eight per cent! You're not serious? That's robbery, in any language!"

"I saw a man nearly get his head blown off, today, because of it." And Tanner gave a terse account of the confrontation between Sam Harolday and the German.

"That must have been the gunshot I heard," Newcome said. "Nobody I talked to seemed to know—but they never mentioned the eight per cent, either. . . . Yeah, I was talking to a few people," he added, "whilst waiting for you. Of course, most I heard I take with a grain of salt—those worthless boomers don't count for nothing. They only flocked here because property in Newton and Wichita was too steep for them—and now, dealing amongst themselves, they've gone and jacked *these* prices out of all reason.

"Their balloon should bust about time the first train pulls in, and we begin to see just how much a twenty-five-foot frontage lot on Railroad Avenue is actually worth. You can count on it—we'll hear cursing and moaning, but it won't take the bulk of that crowd long to melt away and drift on somewheres else, none of them the wiser."

"A town has got to grow normally," Clark Tanner admitted. "This one started on paper. It could die there."

"It's happened," Parley Newcome said. "Plenty of times. But, there's always some other town."

"I suppose. . . ." Tanner was looking at the plate he held in his lap, and after a moment he said slowly, "Only, I don't know if I have the guts left to go hunting the next one."

"That's no way to talk!" Newcome sounded shocked; the protest was jarred out of him. "You're just beat from rassling with that damn press. I am, myself. But, hell! You're a born fighter! Like when you saw that crooked setup there in Nebraska, and went after it on your editorial page."

"And ended up, you sneaking me out of town half dead in the back of a wagon!" Tanner shook his head. "I'm not sure but what I left my fight behind me. I carry the reminder every step I take." It wasn't necessary to explain that he meant the shattered hip—a constant torment.

There was a silence. Parley Newcome scraped up the last of his beans, laid the plate aside. He seemed to be groping for something to lighten the tone of their talk.

"Oh, well," he said finally, "maybe things are due to start breaking better. This Beason character and his partner, I ain't sure I'd trust 'em a minute; but even the ones I heard grumbling had to admit they're working hard to put this town over. At least they haven't been doing the obvious things, like knocking down lots at auction for whatever they could get in a hurry. Instead, they seem to have some money—though nobody seems to know where they got it—and they're plowing it in. Beason's supposed to be building himself a house over on Union; he intends to move there permanent, out of the shack behind the land office where the two of 'em have been batching it.

"So at any rate you got to say they have faith in their own town. Though that still wouldn't inspire me," he added dryly as he hitched to his feet, "to get on the business end of eight per cent interest!"

"Nor me," Tanner said.

He got up and went to stand in the rear doorway. The long dusk of summer lay on this wide Arkansas River bottom. Overhead the sky was gray steel, beginning to prick with stars. The big bulk of the hotel and the other structures, over on Railroad Avenue, cut black silhouettes that were spotted with occasional yellow squares of lamplit windows. A faint breeze stirred, carrying the scorched smells of Kansas earth.

Parley Newcome came up behind him and Clark Tanner said, "Well, we're here now. We've got three months' free rent and print stock for a few issues at least. I guess we'll put out a paper."

"I figured," the older man said.

They stood without speaking to watch as night settled over the empty land and masked this raw beginning of a town incongruously named Eden Grove. . . .

# CHAPTER VI

Hubert Lowndes was a sign painter, a spidery man with straggling whiskers. Tanner found him living in a tent on a vacant lot, surrounded by stacks of unfinished signboards the town's businessmen had contracted for. In return for a bottle of whiskey and the promise of a free ad, Tanner got a sign out of him—a huge one, nearly twelve feet long, bearing in fancy, curlicued letters the legend: EDEN GROVE GAZETTE. When it was finally done—after Lowndes had been made to repaint it because he put in an extra Z—Tanner and Newcome collected it and transported the thing between them through the streets, one carrying either end. Using borrowed ladders they hoisted and nailed their sign across the front of the newspaper office, above the door, and were officially in business.

Later, as he could afford it, Tanner hoped to invest in some boiler plate and increase his *Gazette* to a regulation, four-page format; just now, operating without funds and with less than a week to put a first issue together, he would have to settle for a single sheet, handbill-size, but printed on both faces. And while Parley Newcome labored to put the plant in shape—overhauling and oiling the old flatbed press, separating type, and starting to set copy as his boss got it ready—Clark Tanner took to spending full, eighteen-hour days on the street.

He made the rounds of the business houses, to introduce himself and get acquainted with the new town's merchants. He kept a sharp eye out for new arrivals that looked more promising than the boomers filling the bars on Railroad Avenue—anyone who might be bringing new business. He checked on reports of progress from the end of track, still some twenty miles away but inching nearer up the broad Arkansas valley.

Wherever he could, he promoted ads for the paper. McDougall, at the livery, took one in partial payment for the team and wagon. The hotel owner, Phil Steadman, kept his promise and paid cash in advance for a half-dozen insertions—Tanner didn't know if this really proved the man's confidence in the town and in the *Gazette*, or was merely a charitable gesture; but he was glad enough to accept the money. At least it guaranteed a few more meals for himself and Parley Newcome.

As could be expected, Steadman had his own estimate as to the future of Eden Grove. "A lot of things can affect it," he said to Tanner over drinks at the hotel bar, "including competition from towns that don't even exist yet. Lately I've been hearing word from Fort Dodge—that's a military post, some hundred miles farther west, upriver from us."

"I've heard of it," Tanner said.

"Well, there's a bunch out there has plans, when the Santa Fe builds that far. I admit it worries me some. I know the place; not a bad site for a town, what with the soldiers already there, and maybe a potential for the trade in buffalo hides."

"But you're still an optimist for Eden Grove?"

"Oh, sure. I'm one by nature—or I'd never have got in the hotel business! After all, we'll have a head start. If we can just get some kind of a cattle market established this summer, it could give us three, maybe four years to consolidate before we begin to feel the pressure from Dodge. That ought to be enough. . . ."

Later, discussing what Steadman had said, Parley Newcome sounded skeptical but not too concerned. "All right," he said with a shrug. "We both know any town's a gamble, including this one. So somebody deals it deuces—all we have to do is move on somewhere else, change the name of the paper and sit in on a new hand. Who knows? We might wind up, ourselves, in this Dodge Town or whatever they decide to call it."

"Maybe."

Aside from a natural reluctance over new starts, Clark Tanner was surprised to find in himself a real interest as to the future of this place where he'd cast his lot. His dislike and mistrust of Colby and Beason hadn't grown any the less, the more he saw of them, but there were other people in this town that he did like and could identify with. Phil Steadman, for one, and the doctor, and bald-headed Peter Duffy who ran the New York Restaurant, and Merv Booker at the furniture store. Already he was beginning to think of them as friends.

Others, he didn't quite know what to make of. One was Harolday, the store manager—a man who showed the world an impressive front and manner, yet struck Tanner as missing in some quality which should have made him more than the hired agent for Virgil Beason. Tanner saw him almost daily, but it was toward the end of that first week that he again encountered Harolday's wife.

They met near the store, the woman accompanied by a fair-haired little girl who, at perhaps two years of age, gave every sign of someday being as handsome as her mother. Tanner lifted his hat to them; they exchanged greetings and general comments, and Mrs. Harolday, rather surprisingly, invited him into the family living quarters for a chat. There, after locking the street door, she proceeded to serve him tea and cakes.

He knew that this home was temporary, making do until her husband could put up and furnish a proper one for his family, but Lucy Harolday offered no apology. The little girl sat with them at the table, with her own plate and spoon and glass of milk. The china service and the silverware, which the woman produced with every evidence of pride, looked like prized possessions from a better time; here, they could not have seemed more out of place. Tanner commented on the chinaware and was gratified to see her pleasure.

"They belonged to my mother," she told him, her face aglow. "She brought them home from a visit to New York."

"Where was 'home'?"

"We're from Pennsylvania," Mrs. Harolday said. "A country village back in the west hills. It does seem a long time ago." The smile faded a little.

"I guess there isn't much about this country to remind you of it."

"I don't need anything to remind me. . . ." She shook her head then. "I suppose all of us came from somewhere else. Some are able to adjust better than others." She looked toward the unscreened window, white with the blast of a Kansas summer. Hot wind stirred the curtains, that looked odd against the unfinished lumber of the window frame; but air circulation was poor, the room hot and nearly breathless.

"What bothers me most," Lucy Harolday said, "is not having anyone to talk to. There's just that mob out there on the street, that makes a person almost afraid to step outside her door. Hardly any women at all; and Jeanie is soon going to need other children to play with."

Tanner tried to reassure her. "Wait just a little longer. When the railroad comes, you should begin seeing families arrive on every train. And that will mean churches, and schools, and all the other things families need—the things that will turn this into a town, instead of merely the promise of one."

" 'When the railroad comes,' " she repeated frowning. "That's all anyone ever hears—the only thing we live for. I just hope we know what we're talking about!"

The cakes she had made were good and Tanner let her offer him a second and refill his cup. Afterward she said, "Speaking of families, I was wondering if you knew anything about the Burkhalters? The people who were in the store the other day, when there was some"—she hesitated over the word—"some misunderstanding about their bill. . . ."

"I've heard nothing new," Tanner said. "I suppose it's an occasion, when people like that get in off their homestead. I've thought some of going out to see how they're doing. But I'm really crowded for time these days, trying to put out a first issue."

"Of course." She seemed genuinely interested in his newspaper, and they talked about that awhile. But then, turning the cup in her saucer, she reverted suddenly. "Mr. Tanner, the thing you witnessed that first day—the argument you almost got involved in . . ." She stumbled over whatever she was trying to tell him. "I—I hope you understand my husband is really only an employee here. He doesn't set policy for the store, on matters of credit."

Looking at her sharply, Tanner could have added: *And I suppose he's following orders, when he conveniently forgets to tell his customers about the interest rate on their bills?* But there was no point in that—no need for any answer, just then, for they were interrupted by the sound of the street door opening, and Sam Harolday's voice calling his wife's name.

Harolday sounded angry. A moment later he appeared in the

doorway of the living quarters, holding the key with which he had let himself in. Without preliminary he demanded, irritably, "Why is the store closed in the middle of the afternoon? Don't you know we can be losing money?"

The woman returned his look. "In a half hour or so? I doubt we lose much—They'll come back if there's something they really want." She continued before he had a chance to argue the point: "Jeanie has been shut up in this place too much. We just had to get some fresh air to breathe, Sam. So I took her for a walk, even though there isn't really any place to walk to. And we met Mr. Tanner, and I invited him in for a cup of tea."

Harolday had been eyeing the visitor, and anyone must have been blind to miss the naked suspicion in his face. But then he looked at his little girl, sitting at the table, with a ring of milk about her mouth as she placidly finished her cake and licked frosting off her fingers; and her presence must have done something to reassure him. He took another tack. Still scowling, he gruffly told his wife, "I've said I don't like you and the child going out when I'm not with you. No knowing what you could run into, in a town as raw as this."

Lucy Harolday's head lifted, and there was color in her cheeks as she snapped, "I'm well aware of it!" And Clark Tanner was uneasily conscious of witnessing a skirmish in a continuing war between husband and wife. It would be embarrassing for any man, but particularly for a bachelor; he came at once to his feet, taking his hat from the knob of his chair where he had hung it.

"I've been off the job too long," he said quickly. "Time I was going. Thanks again for the refreshments."

Her answering smile as she said, "You'll come again, won't you?" was brief and almost perfunctory. "If I can," he answered indefinitely, and was relieved to get out of there.

Tanner suspected Sam Harolday was a stuffed shirt, and he felt sympathy and perhaps even pity for his wife; nevertheless he made a mental note that he would never again be caught between them. He had worries enough of his own!

Thursday, July 11, 1872, had been named press day for the first issue of the Eden Grove *Gazette*. No newspaper was ever put to bed without last-minute delays and problems; it was past nine that evening—a hasty supper cleared away, a trace of lemon-yellow light still staining the sky beyond the windows—when Clark Tanner and Parley Newcome rolled up their sleeves and set about getting the old flatbed press into action.

A last few paragraphs had been written and set up and Newcome was working at the stone, locking the forms before inking them and pulling proofs for Tanner's inspection. Suddenly, after days of endless work and growing tension, Clark Tanner's part was nearly over; with nothing for his hands to do, he could only stand by and watch the older man work expertly at the job he knew so well.

The street door opened. Doc Riggs stuck his head in, looking rumpled as usual and carrying his medical bag. Hand on the knob, he watched the activity at the composing table. "Looks like you're putting her to bed."

"Almost," Clark Tanner told him.

"Well, I wouldn't want to interrupt that," the doctor said. "But I thought you ought to know." He hefted the bag. "I've just had a call over to Lew Cotton's place. There's been a knifing."

"A knifing?" Parley Newcome paused with mallet lifted. "A bad one?" Fights as such were no great rarity among the rootless men who crowded the dives on Railroad Avenue. Fists came into use and guns were known to be drawn, but to date there had been no fatalities or even serious injuries.

"All I know, somebody had a blade shoved into him and I'm wanted, fast—before he bleeds to death. Just a row over a game, I suppose; even so, I thought there might be a story in it for you. Well, I've got to go." And Riggs ducked out again, leaving Newcome and Tanner looking at each other.

"A stabbing over a saloon card game," Clark Tanner said with distaste. "Pretty sordid."

"But it's news. And this *is* a newspaper."

"I take it you want to have a look?"

"Why not? I always liked the sight of blood. We're going to be at this job all night, anyway," Newcome pointed out. "We might as well have a break."

Reluctantly Tanner said, "Let's go, then."

They left everything as it was, turned the lamp down, and locked the door behind them. Cotton's, on the west corner of C

Street and a couple of blocks from the print shop, was the biggest saloon on Railroad Avenue but only sketchily equipped as yet, with little more than a cheap plank bar and a few tables and stools for poker players. Hampered as they were by Tanner's game leg, by the time they arrived word had spread and just now the long, low-ceilinged room appeared to contain a good part of the town's floating population; a good knifing would have been a break in the monotony, to bring them flocking in.

For so big a crowd, they weren't making an awful lot of noise as they stood around, waiting for news. A couple of girls, who served Cotton's customers both here in the bar and in their cribs out back, were huddled together and looking frightened. Attention seemed centered on the cubbyhole of an office; through its open door John Riggs could be seen in there, coat off and sleeves rolled up, working over a man stretched out on an army cot, while his friend Phil Steadman and another stood by and held oil lamps to give him the light he needed.

Tanner, looking for information, made his way through the crowd with Parley Newcome at his heels. He found Lew Cotton, elbows back against the bar, a cigar clamped between his jaws. Cotton was a swart, stocky figure with a ferocious black mustache and the beginning of a paunch, probably from years of drinking his own goods in dives like this that he'd operated, in one town or another, across the frontier. "Who is it that got cut?" Tanner asked.

"Name's Fosburg," the saloon owner told him. "Dunno any more than that, except he's been in and out of here swapping deals in building lots and spending his money."

Another boomer. . . . "Did you see what happened?"

"Heard the tail end of it. There was some fuss or other about a discard. Before I could move to break it up a knife got pulled. By him." Cotton pointed with the wet end of his cigar.

Tanner had already located the knifer, seated on a stool at one of the tables, a couple of the men grimly standing guard. He saw considerable blood and, there amid the wreckage of an interrupted game, the knife itself—a nasty-looking tool, bone-handled, needle-sharp.

"Has the look of a tinhorn," Parley Newcome said.

And he did, Tanner agreed—something in the cut of his

clothes, in the well-brushed derby hat lying on the table beside him. The man had thinning, tightly curled black hair and a face trained to reveal no secrets; but there was fear in him now. He was in bad trouble and there was no question that he knew it.

The saloonkeeper said, "Gaddis, I heard somebody say his name is."

"He's not a houseman, then?"

"Oh, hell no. I don't run games here—just take a cut for the cards and the chips. I've seen this fellow around the last day or two, playing anyone who'd sit in with him. He looked harmless."

"You should have run him off, harmless or not," someone commented sternly.

Virgil Beason had come up to join them. "It's the gamblers and grifters and floaters," he pointed out, "that make trouble for a new town if they're allowed to light."

"You'll never keep them out," Lew Cotton told him flatly. "Especially after the railroad hits and they start coming in on the cars. You can count on it."

"It's the Texas trade that will bring them," Parley Newcome added. "They'll be flocking in like carrion crows, same as at Abilene and Ellsworth. The con men and the cardsharks and the whores who work the trail crews can smell money and a wide-open town a hundred miles away."

Beason scowled at him—he seemed to have taken a dislike to Clark Tanner's helper at first meeting, and the feeling gave every sign of being mutual. "Eden Grove is no wide-open town."

"Without laws or any way to enforce them?" Newcome shrugged. "Good luck! Just remember—one killing breeds another."

"No one's dead yet," Beason said crisply. "Riggs seemed to think the man had a chance of pulling through."

At that moment John Riggs straightened from his work, lifting his shoulders to ease the strain from them and letting them drop again. He nodded as if satisfied, signaled for his helpers to remove the lamps they had held for him, and picked up a towel to wipe his hands as he came out into the main room. "Best I can do," he announced. "I've got him sewed up, and there don't seem to be any internal bleeding."

"Will he live?" Virgil Beason demanded.

"Should. A rib deflected the knife point—I've seen men get up and walk away, after being hurt worse. It's the shock that knocked him out." To Lew Cotton the doctor added, "He should stay where he is, for now. Put blankets on him and keep him warm until he comes around."

"I'm stuck with the sonofabitch, am I?" Lew Cotton swore disgustedly but sent his bartender off to fetch the necessary blankets. "Minute he's on his feet," the saloon man said, "out he goes. I ain't running no free flophouse!"

The doctor tossed his towel on the bar with a shrug. "Suit yourself. I'll be around in the morning, to check on how he's doing." And Riggs went back into the office to gather up his tools.

The temper of the crowd had eased to a degree, Tanner thought, when they heard the doctor's verdict; now they watched as Virgil Beason strode over to where the prisoner sat, under guard. "You're in luck, mister," he told the gambler. "You realize this would have been murder?"

Gaddis, with head tilted back, retorted, "Like hell! He called me a cheat and came after me. I had a right to defend myself."

Beason flapped a hand, contemptuously. "Nobody's interested in your excuses. I just want to hear how long it will take you to get yourself out of this town!"

One of the guards was a big man with the red-veined face of a heavy drinker; he demanded in quick protest, "You saying we should turn the bastard loose?"

"What do *you* want to do?" Beason retorted sharply, as the buzz of talk in the room gradually quieted. "Take him out and hang him, I suppose—give Eden Grove the reputation of a lynching town! *That* would be a great start, wouldn't it? Do a lot for property values!"

He let this roomful of speculators chew the thought for a moment. "Is it what you want?" Beason repeated, driving the point home.

The guard was forced to break gaze, stammering a little. "Hell!" he muttered roughly. "I only thought—"

"You *didn't* think," Virg Beason corrected him coldly and turned back to the prisoner. "I asked you a question."

The gambler answered quickly. "Mister, I got a horse at the livery. Won't take but about five minutes to throw a saddle on and be out of this damned town—and I hope I never see the place again!"

"For your own hide's sake, you had better make sure!"

Beason jerked his head toward the street door, and Gaddis got hurriedly to his feet. But Phil Steadman had emerged from the office in time to hear this. He blew the lamp he'd been holding, to assist his friend Riggs, and placed it on the bar. He said, "Let's not go too fast. According to the law, this man may still be guilty of attempted murder. He ought to be turned over to the authorities."

"You want to do it?" Beason retorted. "It's over forty miles to Hutchinson. And what makes you think the sheriff would want us bothering him with some argument over a poker game?"

Steadman considered that. He rubbed his jaw as he looked at the prisoner. "All right," he said finally. "If John had any real doubt about the man he knifed pulling through, I'd damn well insist on hanging on to him. But I suppose it would only be a nuisance. So, go on," he told the gambler. "Do like he said. Get out —while we're in the mood to let you."

Gaddis snatched up his bowler. For a moment his glance touched on the knife lying on the table; Steadman said crisply, "Leave that!" A look around him must have convinced the gambler not to make an issue of it. He drew himself up, with a contemptuous stare for the crowd. But to Clark Tanner it looked as though the hand that placed the bowler on his head was trembling more than a little.

In a dead silence the gambler passed down the long room to the door. Hostile looks followed him, but no one said a word, or lifted a hand to stop him as they drew back to let him through. Then he was gone, the louvered doors clacking shut behind him; his footsteps sounded on the wooden gallery.

But when he hit the short stretch of boardwalk at the foot of the steps, Gaddis was running.

# CHAPTER VII

Gaddis left controversy behind him, though most of the crowd—turning back to normal activities—was unaware of it. Lew Cotton, having appropriated the wicked-looking knife before, he said, some other damn fool should get his hands on it and do more mischief, was busy overseeing his bartender in cleaning up the bloody mess created by the stabbing. But at the bar Phil Steadman and his friend Riggs were locked in argument with Virgil Beason. It seemed to Tanner, listening to their voices raised above the noise around them, that a long-smoldering dispute had finally come into the open.

John Riggs had cleaned up and packed his bag, and now he was pouring himself a drink. Tanner heard the doctor exclaiming angrily, "So nobody was killed—but what about next time, and the one after that? I'm not always going to be lucky enough to patch these fools up after they get through with each other, even if I did manage tonight. Sooner or later there's going to be killings, especially if we get this town full of wild Texas cowhands, drunk and five hundred miles from home."

"That's right!" Steadman agreed. "Tonight just proves the thing I've been saying all along: We need law here, and some kind of government to enforce it. We've got to stop dragging our feet before it's too late, and get this town organized under legal statute."

Beason said, frozen-faced, "I don't know that anyone's dragging their feet."

"No?" Steadman snapped it up. "Only last month I circulated a petition of organization and couldn't get more than a half-dozen signatures. I kept hearing the same arguments, but mostly it came down to one thing—money! They weren't ready for any real government if it meant costing them some taxes."

Beason lifted a shoulder. "It's understandable. You can't expect a man to be in any hurry about voting a levy on his own income, no matter in how good a cause."

"You didn't sign either," John Riggs pointed out. "Or your partner."

"No, we didn't—because we could see that petition wasn't getting anywhere. With no more signatures than you had," Beason said, patiently, as though to men who couldn't recognize the obvious, "any court would have thrown the thing back in our faces. You've got to learn that people have to be led. They won't be pushed!"

The doctor's mild brown eyes, behind thick lenses, had been quietly studying the man as he talked. Now, without raising his own voice, John Riggs said, "I don't call any man a liar, Beason; but I think there were other reasons they wouldn't sign. One of those men—I won't tell you his name—but, afterwards, he same as admitted he'd wanted to but didn't dare. He was warned by somebody he owed money to."

Beason was staring at him; a slow spot of color began to show on either prominent cheekbone. "Do you mean me, by any chance?" he demanded, in a voice that was suddenly not quite under control. "Are you saying I used threats to stop that petition?"

"I'm only saying what I was told."

"Nat Colby and I built Eden Grove from nothing. Maybe you can suggest one reason why either of us would want to hold it back."

Riggs met his angry look. "I might."

"You wouldn't want to spell that out?" the other challenged, his lips tight.

The doctor shook his head. "I don't think so."

The sharp eyes continued to spear him for a moment, though Riggs seemed wholly unperturbed. Finally Beason said, in a voice roughened by emotion, "And I don't think I care for your riddles!" As though not trusting himself to say more, he turned abruptly and left them, elbowing men out of his way. They watched him go, after which Phil Steadman turned to the doctor with a look of concern.

Steadman told his friend, "You pushed him pretty hard."

"Long as I'm the only doctor this town of his has got," Riggs said coolly, "he needs me—and after tonight he knows it!" He drained off the drink he'd poured, took his instrument bag from the bartop. "I must be getting old. A little job like the one I just did on that fellow in the other room shouldn't take the spit out of me. Meanwhile there's a drummer at the hotel that apparently got ahold of some bad booze somewhere; I promised to look in on him."

"I'll come with you," Steadman said. He looked at Tanner and Newcome. "You staying?"

Tanner gave his head a shake. "Not us. We've still got a paper to put to bed. . . ."

Afterward, as they walked together along the darkened street, the older man suiting his stride to the other's awkward crippled gait, Parley Newcome asked in a casual tone, "Did you catch the drift of the doc's riddles?"

"Did you?"

"Oh, I figure it was plain enough. Beason and Colby dug this puddle and right now they're the king frogs. They're afraid they might not always be, once the town gets organized under the law. Virg Beason would like nothing better than to stall until he's sure he can control any government that gets set up." Newcome gave his boss a sideward look in the darkness of the street. "You've been around town long as I have, and God knows you're smarter than me. I shouldn't have to tell you this!"

Clark Tanner, thoughtfully silent, made no answer.

At the print shop, everything was as they had left it, in readiness, the forms for the two pages locked and waiting to be set into the press. Tanner went about turning up the lamps and propping open the doors for better circulation of air. But when he returned he found Parley Newcome had done nothing about setting up for the run.

Newcome was looking over the forms, reading type in reverse rather than bothering to look at the page proofs. Now he said, "Here's some filler on page two we can do without. Jerking that and moving stuff around should give you maybe a half column on the first page. Is that enough?" And when his boss only looked at him he added quickly, "We're gonna be putting in something about this business tonight at Cotton's, ain't we?"

Tanner frowned. "A brawl in a saloon? That's hardly my idea of news."

"Maybe not. But what about the talk that came out of it? For the good of the town, it deserves an airing. Hell, we both know Steadman and the doc are right—and Beason's dead wrong. And you're the man who can make the issue clear. I figure you got a duty!"

As Clark Tanner considered, sounds of the night bore in upon them—the rise and fall of the cicada chorus, the carrying racket from the saloons on Railroad Avenue. Slowly Tanner shook his head.

"It's too late in the day," he said shortly, "to be tearing up the whole format. I guess we'll just go with what we have."

"But—" Newcome's protest died unfinished. Tanner could hardly miss the disappointment in the older man's stare; he simply turned away from it, not waiting for an argument.

Grudgingly, plainly disapproving, Parley Newcome said roughly then, "It's your paper. Let's put it to bed. . . ."

Tanner awoke feeling almost hungover, as though in the aftermath of a drinking bout; he knew it was only an accumulation of fatigue and long hours and the letting down of tension, the deadline of press day met and passed. He opened eyes that burned as though gritty with sand, lay a moment befuddled and disoriented. The fog inside his skull cleared then and he knew where he was, and the month and the day of the week.

Stoically prepared for the stab of pain in his sleep-stiffened bad hip, he pushed up and swung his legs over the edge of the cot and looked across the room at Parley Newcome. Newcome lay on his back, his mouth open, snoring softly. The stub of white whiskers on sunken cheeks gave him the look just then of a very old man, exhausted by the hard use life had made of him. Tanner looked at him for a minute or two.

He got his feet under him then and limped over to the washstand, and felt better when he had splashed water over his face and head. He pulled on his trousers and padded, barefooted, out into the main room of the print shop.

After last night's busy activity it seemed oddly still. In the midst of everything, the old press had broken down and had to have emergency repair; now it stood idle and motionless and silent. On the worktable he could see the end result of his and Parley Newcome's hours of labor—a neat stack of finished newspapers, each a single sheet, six columns wide and printed on both sides. When Tanner picked the top one off the pile, the ink was still pungently fresh. Though he had written it all, he stood now in the silent room and read quickly down the columns, with a professional's ability to see his own words with a fresh eye.

Not too bad a job, he told himself—well set up, cleanly printed, with a fair balance of text and advertising. There was a congratulatory card from each of the town's businesses, though not all of these had been paid for or were likely to be—Tanner had run them anyway. The news stories had as their one theme a positive and optimistic report of Eden Grove, daily growing and looking confidently to the future.

But even as he nodded in satisfaction, Clark Tanner felt a nagging trouble and recognized its source—the disapproving look on Parley Newcome's face last evening as he scanned the first copy off the press. Suddenly Tanner swore.

"Doesn't the man know he's wrong?" he muttered angrily. "He's been in this business long enough; he saw what happened in Nebraska. There's a time for stirring up controversy—and there's also a time when a newspaper can destroy itself. If Parley Newcome doesn't like it—" He left the thought unfinished, bitterness in the set of his mouth.

He had done the best he knew; it would have to stand. With a shrug he dropped the sheet of paper back upon the table. For better or worse, the Eden Grove *Gazette* was off the press; there only remained to see it distributed.

Tanner dressed and shaved without disturbing the sleeping Parley Newcome, who could be dead except for the sound, halfway between a groan and a muffled snore, that came now and then from his slack and gaping mouth. Tanner left him sleeping and, not bothering about breakfast, took an armload of the printed sheets and let himself out of the shop.

Morning was still new, and Railroad Avenue looked strangely deserted; it would be another hour or two before the sounds of saw and hammer began again, and before the boomers, after a boozy night, came out of their holes to resume their frenetic and pointless swarming. Some places of business were still closed. At the hotel, Tanner found Steadman's nephew, a lanky redhead named Barney Osgood, straightening up the lobby and having to work around the legs of snoring men sprawled in overstuffed chairs and on the sofa. Clark Tanner deposited a number of newspapers on the desk, where they would be sold to Steadman's customers; as he left, the young night clerk had knocked off work to read Eden Grove's first newspaper, while he yawned and scratched at his tangled hair.

Duffy's New York Restaurant—an impressive name for a five-stool, two-table eat shack—was almost the only place along the street actually doing business this early. Peter Duffy was at work over his stove behind the counter, a jovial, sweating tub of a man in grease-spattered undershirt, who returned Tanner's greeting with a grin and a wave of the spatula he was using to turn flapjacks on the griddle. His only customers at the moment were seated at one of the tables—the liveryman, Tom McDougall, and Merv Booker who ran the furniture store; the latter was pouring syrup onto a plate of cakes. Tanner gave them each a paper on his way to hitch a seat at the counter. There, well aware of the limited menu, he said, "I'll take a stack of those. And coffee."

"You bet." Duffy was not in the least bothered by the heat from the blazing stove. He mopped a sheen of moisture from his completely bald head and brought a fistful of silverware and a china cup, which he filled from the steaming iron pot. He saw the printed sheets Tanner had set on the counter; he exclaimed, "Hey, is this what I think it is? Let's have a look!" and helped himself to one. Being farsighted he had to hold it at arm's length and crane his head well back, while he turned to get the best light. "Well!" he said. "Looks to me, the town finally has itself an honest-to-God newspaper."

Clark Tanner said, "It's what I was aiming for."

"Where's my ad?" Tanner pointed, and Duffy blew out bulbous cheeks as he examined it critically. "I always wondered how my name would look in print!" He had to put the paper aside and hurry back to his stove, then, to turn his cakes and pour fresh dollops of batter from a white china pitcher.

Clark Tanner stirred sugar and cream into his coffee, while he waited, and watched his two fellow customers silently reading their copies of the *Gazette*.

He tried to find some reaction in their faces. Tom McDougall's gaunt features had settled into a look that might be distaste or only concentration; Booker for his part had the kind of bland, round face, festooned with Dundreary whiskers, that seldom showed anything. A stranger might have thought Merv Booker stupid; having seen the man in the surroundings of his furniture establishment, and had some talk with him, Tanner was quite certain there was nothing stupid about him. Actually there was some air of mystery: Nobody seemed to know where he had come from, or what he thought about most matters. He seldom said very much, and he hid his intelligence behind eyes that reflected little.

Flapjacks sizzled on the fire, and Peter Duffy flipped them deftly onto a couple of plates, set one in front of Tanner and carried the other to the table for Tom McDougall. Growing sounds of morning came with the hot wind through the open door as Clark Tanner poured blackstrap on his cakes and began to cut them up.

Getting no response from the men at the table, who were eating now as they read what he had written without any show of enthusiasm, he was suddenly overwhelmed by a sense of failure. All at once he heard himself apologizing and hating himself for it: "I know—the paper doesn't look like much as yet, but I'm just getting started. After another issue or two—if I can pick up some advertising and subscriptions . . ."

Surprisingly, it was Merv Booker who interrupted him, saying with a trace of amusement, "No call to get touchy about it, Tanner. Everybody here is in the same boat, just hanging on and hoping for business to grow. I'd say you'd made a good beginning."

Tom McDougall nodded agreement. "Not bad at all, actually. It's true you've been spending a lot of time with Doc Riggs, and that fellow Steadman—a couple of real soreheads; I half expected the thing to be full of nothing but their opinions."

Tanner felt his cheeks stiffen. "I always said I hoped to be objective."

"I know what you *said*." The liveryman tapped a bony finger on the paper beside his plate. "That's why I'm glad to see this lead story on Beason and Colby. It's only fair that credit should go to the ones responsible for the town even being here."

Peter Duffy, leaning behind his counter, had been reading one of the papers. "Oh, yeah," he said dryly. "No question about it—them two really ought to like this!" Tanner gave him a look, feeling the sharp bite of sarcasm. It stung the harder, coming from this good-natured man whom he had never heard voice the mildest criticism of anyone.

McDougall went on as though he hadn't heard. "I'm glad, too, to see the trouble at Cotton's saloon last night didn't get spread across the front page. I wouldn't have thought any newspaperman could resist it."

Tanner shrugged. "I'm not all that anxious to sell papers. If the man had died, I suppose I'd have had to print something."

"Any word on him?" Duffy wanted to know.

"Riggs wasn't in his office. But when I stopped in at Cotton's I was told the man had lasted through the night. I imagine he's going to make it."

"And the other one, that did the cuttin'? He left town, did he?" Duffy looked at the livery-stable owner, and McDougall nodded.

"Last night. Took his horse and cleared out without paying his bill—and good riddance! At any rate, the incident's closed."

The fat man folded freckled arms on the counter and leaned on them. "That's all right, but supposing somebody *had* died? I'm wondering what we'd have done—took up a collection and shipped him somewheres?"

"Notified the next of kin, I guess," Tanner said. "If we knew of any. And held the body for instructions."

"Not in this weather! We'd have to get him under the ground pretty damn quick. Question is, where would we bury him? People here can die, same as any other place; but far as I know, nobody's so much as thought about a cemetery. And even supposing we had one set aside—who's to do the burying?"

Merv Booker, who as usual had had little to say, dropped knife and fork into his empty plate now. "It's not a subject I'd pick to talk about over breakfast," he remarked, "but when we need use of a cemetery I imagine we'll find one; up there on the bluff might be a likely place. As for the rest, I haven't aired the matter, but it happens I've already sent order in for some boxes, just to have on hand. Seems a natural enough sideline for a furniture dealer. And since we don't have an undertaker, somebody has to volunteer. . . ."

On that sober note the talk ended.

# CHAPTER VIII

Having left a supply of papers with McDougall and Booker to distribute to their customers, Clark Tanner had one more stop to make. Morning was getting older now, the town coming alive. The saws and hammers were starting up, here and there, building the town. Many of the mob of boomers, hungover as usual and irritable from the night before, would be making directly for the saloons to begin the day's drinking, but a few straggled into the New York Restaurant. When Tanner left it, Peter Duffy was busy at his stove frying griddle cakes in a cloud of steam and heat. And every man waiting to be served at the counter and the tables had grabbed himself a copy of the *Gazette*.

Day started early at the town company office. Nat Colby sat at his desk, writing something, and the black-haired clerk was inking changes on the wall map, recording recent sales of lots. They both looked up as Tanner halted in the doorway to ask, "Is Beason around?"

"Hasn't come in yet," Colby answered; but when Tanner moved to withdraw the man stopped him. "What have you got there?" He put down his pen and crooked a thick finger, beckoning.

Tanner keenly resented being summoned in that way, but with a shrug he went and laid the remainder of his papers on the desk, saying briefly, "Make sure he gets these when he comes in." And he watched Nat Colby pick up one of the sheets with a look almost of distaste.

The clerk, too, had left his work to come over and help himself to a copy. His name was Fred Wolters, and on the first day he had got on the wrong side of Tanner with his superior manner; now, chin tilted by his tight, high collar, he ran a supercilious eye over the printed words and the faint curl on his lip indicated what he apparently thought of them. A brief glance at the reverse side, and he tossed the paper down again and went back to his map, without a word. Tanner could gladly have hit him.

Nat Colby had been laboriously following his finger down half a column, and Tanner thought he could see the thick lips move as he read. It was the story about himself that he was going over so painfully, and seeing his scowl Clark Tanner was finally moved to ask, "What's wrong, Colby? You find some mistakes?"

The man shook his head, still reading. "No mistakes," he grunted finally. He sounded almost puzzled as, grudgingly, he admitted, "This ain't too bad, as a matter of fact. Which I must say surprises me, Tanner, because I don't trust none of you educated newspaper fellers. You're that slick, you can make fun of somebody without him even knowing."

Tanner passed that off. "I'm glad you're satisfied—though I never expect to please everybody." He shot a pointed look at Fred Wolters but the clerk, busy shading in squares on the wall map, never felt it.

Colby, hunched over his desk, lifted meaty shoulders. "Well . . . you newspaper fellers!" he repeated heavily; it was plainly a sore subject. "There was one come out from Wichita, couple months ago. I give a solid half hour answering his questions, and then—"

The door opened and Virgil Beason entered, moving briskly as he generally did. He seemed in a good mood. He had a copy of the *Gazette* that he had picked up somewhere; when he saw Tanner he nodded genially and said, "Ah—here's the man now!" He held up the paper. "I must say I'm pleased with this—really pleased." When he saw his cousin with another copy in front of him he added, "What about you, Nat? Wouldn't you agree?"

"I guess." Colby didn't sound enthusiastic. "I was just telling him about that reporter from Wichita—"

Beason waved that aside. "Forget the man from Wichita; we got our own paper now. . . ." He picked up the ones Tanner had placed on the desk, flipped their corners with his thumb. "These aren't all you're leaving me?"

"All I had left," Tanner said.

"It's not enough—not nearly enough." Beason shook his head, tossed them down again. "I'll need a thousand more."

"A thousand!"

"That many every week until I give you further notice. I intend to plaster the whole area—let the world know Eden Grove is on the map."

Clark Tanner hesitated. "To tell the honest truth, I don't have the stock for print runs that size."

"Then, get it! Didn't I say I was financing this?"

"Well, yes. But—"

Beason didn't seem to notice his reluctance. "Figure out what you'll need," he said crisply. "Make up your order. I'll take it to Hutchinson with me tomorrow, when I go, and see that it's put on the wire."

Wolters, the clerk, had a suggestion. "Why not get some boiler plate while you're at it?"

"What the hell's boiler plate?" Nat Colby wanted to know.

"It comes already printed up with recipes and stuff like that. You fill the two outside pages, and it gives you something that at least looks like a four-page paper. Better than the cheap-looking handbill you got there," he added, with a hint of a sneer that Tanner pretended not to notice.

Beason pursed his lips. He looked at Tanner. "Is that right? Can we get some of that?"

"If you want to pay for it. Might take a few weeks."

"Order it. Meanwhile I want a thousand more of these, on whatever stock is available. Have them here tomorrow morning—I want to leave by ten sharp."

Clark Tanner nodded. "They'll be ready. . . ."

He had hurried faster than he liked, getting back across town to the print shop, and his damaged hip was aching sharply. Parley Newcome wouldn't normally take it on himself to break up the page forms without waiting for orders, but all the same it came as a relief to see them on the composing table, still intact. Newcome was sweeping out, raising dust into the hot bars of sunlight flooding through the windows; he paused to watch, as Tanner hung his hat on a wall nail and went limping to the littered table that served him for a desk. "Well?" the old man asked. "How did things seem to go?"

"The paper? Good enough. I got rid of all the copies I took with me."

"People have been dropping by here," Newcome said. "We're just about sold out. Doc Riggs was in and got one."

"Have any comment?"

"Not really—he was off somewhere in a hurry. I asked about the fellow that got knifed. Doc said he'll pull through."

Tanner nodded absently. "I saw Beason and Colby. They both liked our first issue."

"No damn reason they shouldn't!" Parley Newcome said gruffly; Clark Tanner caught the note of disapproval but pretended he didn't.

"We have a job to do," he said, and told of the order for a thousand-copy overrun.

"What the hell does Beason think he wants with that many?"

"He apparently has some way in mind to distribute them. Long as *we're* not being asked to do it—and he's footing the bill—then it's fine with me! Anyway, it appears he's going to be wanting this every week, for the time being."

"All right." Parley Newcome lifted his shoulders, an indifferent shrug. "Might as well get at it—I don't feel much like working all night again!"

Clark Tanner looked at him unhappily as the old man put his broom aside and began to busy himself replacing one of the forms in the hand press. Things between them were not going well, and right now Tanner had no idea what to do about it. He wasn't even sure the two of them were any longer communicating.

And so one more day of blistering summer heat dragged its length, to the monotonous sound of the old press grinding away at the overrun of the Eden Grove *Gazette*. Toward sunset, after a hurried meal and with the job mostly done, Tanner left his printer to finish up alone while he made his customary tour of Railroad Avenue, checking for any late-breaking news and for further reaction to the first issue of his paper. When he returned it was to find they had visitors—Phil Steadman and John Riggs.

"We thought it wasn't right," Riggs told him, "to let our town launch its first newspaper without some kind of a celebration, so we dropped by for the christening."

Steadman held up a bottle. "By rights it calls for champagne, but I did what I could. This is the best I've got in stock; maybe it will do."

Tanner was really touched—such a friendly gesture as this was the last thing he'd have expected. He thanked them both and invited them to make themselves comfortable, while Parley Newcome said, "I'll get something for us to drink out of."

There was little enough in the way of chairs; Tanner hurried to clear the junk from a couple of packing crates. John Riggs was saying, "We wanted you to know we really think you got your paper off to a damn good start." And Steadman added, "Here's what I collected at the hotel desk." It was little more than a dollar, in small change; but every cent of hard cash was welcome.

Then Newcome was back, having managed to scare up three china cups and a tumbler. Clark Tanner felt a twinge of apprehension, seeing he had fetched one for himself; but he held his tongue—Newcome was a grown man and he had every right to join the celebrating.

Phil Steadman uncorked his bottle. Toasts were given, cups raised in salute. They drank and the hotel man poured seconds. Having drained off his first shot, Parley Newcome took his refilled cup into a corner of the room and Tanner saw him settle there on the floor with it, by himself.

Steadman wanted to know about the overrun Newcome had told him was on order for Virg Beason. They speculated as to the use Beason intended making of them. "He's ambitious," Doc Riggs commented dryly, "I'll say that for him! Should be enough copies to plaster everything betwixt here and the Mississippi River. Well—who knows? Maybe they'll get results."

"Let's hope so," Steadman agreed.

Sunset died and, slowly, dusk began to settle. As they mellowed to the taste of good whiskey, the talk became freer—except for Parley Newcome, who sat alone in his corner and said nothing at all. At one point the doctor remarked, "I was out to the Burkhalter place today. I don't think that woman has really been well since her last baby came. The family all work hard, but they're none of them getting the right diet—hardly enough of anything to hold their bodies together."

Steadman suggested, "Maybe, through the paper, we could get up some money for them."

"No." Riggs shook his head emphatically. "Emil Burkhalter would never accept charity—I know him too well even to suggest it. He only brings himself to let me donate my services because he has sense enough to see his wife's health has to come before his stiff-necked German pride. . . ."

The room grew darker; a rasping chorus of cicadas began and swelled, over in the timber along the creek. At some point Parley Newcome, who had been almost forgotten, suddenly reared to his feet and, without saying a word, headed for the door. Tanner started to call after him, changed his mind. As they heard his footsteps move away, Phil Steadman asked, puzzled, "What's eating your friend? He's been acting mighty strange."

"A little disagreement," Tanner said. "Nothing important. Sometimes he gets like that when he's had a drink or two."

"I didn't realize! Maybe it was a mistake, bringing this bottle. . . ."

"He'll be all right."

Twice in the year the man had worked for him, Tanner had seen Parley Newcome slide off the wagon; both times he had come out of it after a week or two, sick and shaking, and in desperate depths of self-disgust from which it took tremendous effort to raise him. He could only hope nothing like that was starting now.

Conversation became more sporadic, interspersed by the clink of the bottle's neck on china. When it grew too dark to see what they were doing, Tanner got up to find a lamp and start it burning; but that somehow appeared to signal a halt to the activities and brought his guests to their feet. Steadman put the cork on what was left in the bottle and set it on the worktable. There were handshakes, a last round of congratulations on the launching of the *Gazette*. Then Riggs and Steadman left, and Tanner was alone.

He hadn't realized it, but he thought he must be a little drunk. He was one who seldom got any real lift from whiskey, yet had the benefit of all the unpleasant side effects—confused thinking, unsteady movements, and a stiff tongue. He carried his lamp into the back room, splashed cold water over his head to clear it. Afterward he kicked off his shoes and, otherwise fully dressed, stretched out to stare at the ceiling and feel the day's heat, trapped there, press down at him. He lay listening to the night's sounds.

Sleep was out of the question; he found he was too conscious of that other, empty bed across the room. At last, with a curse, he sat up and put his shoes on again. He rose and blew the lamp and got his hat as he went out through the print shop and locked the door behind him.

The night air felt almost cool against his flushed face, though there was not a hint of breeze.

He knew of only two or three places to look for Parley Newcome, and he found him on the first try. Newcome was at Cotton's, sitting alone at a rear table with a bottle and glass. He seemed completely oblivious of the hubbub going on, and at first he did not even look up as Tanner came limping to stand looking down at him. But then he did raise his head, and in the light of the oil lamps Tanner saw the unnatural shine of the old man's eyes, the telltale slackness of his features. Clark Tanner said accusingly, "You walked out on the party."

The other lifted a shoulder. "I got my own party."

"So I see." Tanner eyed the bottle, almost a third empty. "You planning to drink all that?"

"Plenty more at the bar if you want some."

"I've had all I need." He added quietly, "And I think you have, too."

"I figure to be the judge of that!" And, defensively, Parley Newcome seized the bottle and clutched it closer as though expecting the other man to take it away from him.

Clark Tanner stood a moment, debating; there was probably no use arguing with a man in his cups, and yet he could not let the matter go. On an impulse he drew out a stool for himself and put his elbows on the table. "Look!" he said, as earnestly as he could manage. "You know that, for you, that stuff is pure poison. You'll tell me it's none of my business—but I owe you too much to stand by and let you do this to yourself, after you'd been managing so well. Now, let's have it out. What's bothering you?"

Parley Newcome glowered. The liquor had put spots of color into both sagging cheeks, but otherwise his face was pallid. His lips trembled as he said, "Let it alone, Tanner. Get the hell away and let *me* alone."

"No." He shook his head. "I can't, because I'm involved in this. Nothing's been right between us from the day we hit this town—and it's been getting worse. But if what you're doing is some crazy attempt to punish me, it just doesn't make any sense."

The other man couldn't hold his stare. He let it drop to the glass clutched in a tight-knuckled grip. "I ain't talking to you right now," he grumbled, and made a move to rise. Tanner, who was still feeling his own drinks, knew a warm rush of anger and he wasn't gentle about it as he caught Newcome by a shoulder and forced him back.

"Oh, yes you are, damn it! Not talking has got us nowhere—but it hasn't stopped you making it clear you disapprove of every single thing I'm doing! Because of what I put, or wouldn't put, in that damned paper, you're convinced I've gone and sold out!"

"Well, ain't you?" Parley Newcome retorted loudly; neither seemed to remember just then they were in a public place, though actually there was little risk of being overheard above the saloon's noisy racket. From a depth of bitterness, the older man continued: "Was a time, I thought my boss the greatest man I ever knew. The way he waded in to fight the dirty politics in that Nebraska town almost made me ashamed for the waste I'd made of my own life. I'd have died for that man! But you ain't him—not any longer.

"Can't blame *you* for that, of course. It took Morg DuShane's bullet to cut you down to size. But wasn't just your leg he crippled! Now, when I see you knuckling to a cheap conniver like Virg Beason, I have to live with the fact that the man I work for is a coward. . . ."

Stung, Clark Tanner lumbered to his feet—too hastily, for it started his head to spinning; he had to clutch at the table edge for balance while the stool he had been sitting on went tumbling over. Speech was torn from him: "I guess you know what you can do about it! By the same token, maybe I can find myself a printer who'll stay sober long enough to set my copy and not continually give me drunken arguments!"

Parley Newcome looked as though he had been struck in the face. He stared at Tanner, his mouth agape; he closed it finally, swallowed once, and slowly nodded. "All right." The words came out in a mumble, barely audible. "I'll be in tomorrow and pick up my stuff."

"I owe you wages," Tanner said coldly. "I'll raise the money somehow."

They glared at each other a moment longer. Abruptly, Tanner heeled about and strode away from there, leaving Parley Newcome hunched over his bottle and his glass. He did not look back.

It was the tormenting strike of sunlight directly into his eyes that roused him. Grimacing, Tanner moved his head on the pillow in a vain attempt to escape, and flung up a protecting arm—only gradually did he come awake enough to understand how late he must have slept for the sun to be hanging directly above the window by his cot.

Now, too, he became aware of someone moving about, out in the main room of the shop, and of a tantalizing odor which he identified as coffee brewing. Slowly thoughts and memories began to fall into place, like rugged and unwieldy blocks. When at last he stirred himself and tried to sit up, the pounding in his skull made him realize, *I must have drunk more than I knew!* There came a distinct impression of himself standing in the door of the print shop, killing off what was left of the whiskey Phil Steadman had brought and then sending the bottle spinning, end for end, into the night.

Suppressing a groan, he managed to get his feet on the floor and saw he had on underwear and trousers. He pushed to a stand and went out into the main room.

The noise he had heard was the sound of a broom in the hands of Parley Newcome, at his customary morning job of sweeping out. Newcome looked years older, gray and hollow-eyed and haggard. He returned Tanner's nod.

"You should have woke me," Tanner said. "What time is it?"

Newcome paused in his work to drag out an ancient railroad watch and squint at the dial. "Little after nine."

Tanner swore. He found a tin cup and helped himself to some of the black coffee brewing on the stove; he made a face over it, but it served to clear his head somewhat. Drinking he watched the older man at his work. As he set the empty cup aside he said, "Well, I better get dressed; I promised to deliver that extra run to

Beason's office by ten o'clock. We won't be needing the forms again," he continued. "Go ahead and break them up. And then," he indicated the old hand press, "take another look and see if we haven't got a replacement for that bolt that kept coming loose yesterday."

"All right," Parley Newcome said. Clark Tanner went to finish dressing.

Neither mentioned what had been said last night, over the table in Cotton's saloon. By tacit agreement, each knew it would never be spoken of again.

# CHAPTER IX

It looked as though things were beginning to move.

At the hotel bar, Tanner and Steadman had a talk with a couple of strangers. They appeared oddly alike, those two, for men who were plainly not related. In their dusty and trail-worn clothing, they had an identical, fined-down look as though every spare scrap of flesh had been pared away. Their lean and weather-beaten faces bore pale squint lines at the eye corners, from peering into fierce suns and plains winds. The ponies they had left tied to Steadman's hitch rail were equally tough and rawboned, the double-cinched saddles and gear bearing the scars from long and hard use. And in contrast with Kansas speech, they talked with a slurred drawl that could only mean Texas.

These were Mart Niblo and Pen Hansford, his *segundo*, with three thousand head of beef, trail-branded Rafter 7, that they'd brought up from San Saba County bound for Ellsworth. Last evening they'd crossed the Arkansas at a point some ten miles to the east, and now the herd was being held a day before making the final push to the Kansas Pacific market; meanwhile, hearing of a new town, Niblo had fancied a look at it and ridden the extra distance for that purpose, as well as to pick up needed supplies.

There was a lot of interest, according to Niblo, in this place with the fancy name of Eden Grove. News had its mysterious ways of traveling. Just now the drives that followed old Jesse Chisholm's trail were still pointing farther east and north; but once word passed down the grapevine that the rails had been laid here and cars were actually available at the shipping pens, then they could depend on it—later herds would be bending that trail westward for the sake of the few days to be saved. And if the first outfits liked what they found, there would be more before this summer was through.

Why not, Phil Steadman suggested, be the first? The rails would surely arrive inside the month. Niblo could throw his herd on open range of good, untouched buffalo grass and be fattening them up while he waited, likely make a profit over what he would realize by continuing on to Ellsworth. The Texan considered, but shook his head. "I guess not. Happens I've already got a buyer waiting who'll give me top dollar. But next year, maybe."

They shook hands all around, and before pulling out Niblo ordered a couple of bottles to put in his saddle bags and take back for the crew. Steadman wouldn't let him pay. "That's just to remind you," he said, "Texas gets a fair shake in Eden Grove. . . ."

Later that same day there was a flurry of real excitement; this time it was a pair of heavy wagons that lumbered into town, one loaded with bulky timbers and the other holding a dozen tough, hardhanded men who at once piled out and scattered noisily for the nearest saloon. It was a bridge crew, sent by the railroad to throw a trestle over the creek and knock together something to serve as a temporary depot. Their foreman placed the steel gang approximately ten days behind them—which meant, if schedules were maintained, the first Santa Fe cars could be expected to roll in within three weeks or less.

It took perhaps five minutes for the word to spread through this scatter of staked lots and empty streets and tents and raw-lumber buildings, and bring nearly every man on the townsite flocking to hear for himself the first tangible news of progress. It seemed to work like an injection directly into the town's bloodstream, quickening its sluggish pulse. Moreover, as the tempo of things picked up, one could almost have begun to believe in a grapevine such as Mart Niblo had spoken about.

For all at once the world outside, too, appeared aware and interested. Clark Tanner didn't know whether the *Gazette* could claim any credit for the way in which, overnight, the stream of wagons and saddle horses bringing curious new arrivals to Eden Grove virtually doubled. There were campfires now, in the dusk along the river bottom. And now, for the first time, a few buildings were starting to go up south of the right-of-way, facing those already lining Railroad Avenue.

Nat Colby was in his element. With Virgil Beason off on another business trip, it left him the only partner on the townsite; his florid face gleamed with sweat and self-importance as he bustled about, everywhere at once, shaking hands and buying drinks and showing lots to possible customers. Tanner paid him little mind, having doubts as to how impressed any responsible businessman would be with Nat Colby—certainly, the ones he favored seemed to run to small-time operators of the same stripe as himself and his cousin, Virgil Beason. There were others, in Tanner's view, who held much more promise for solid value and real contribution to the growth of a new town.

For the town *was* growing; the hammers kept up their work, and one by one buildings were being finished to fill the gaps in the line-up of business houses. During this past week a drugstore, its show window displaying the usual globes of colored liquids, had opened on the corner of C Street, east across the intersection from Cotton's saloon. Farther along Railroad Avenue, an aggressive young merchant named Bob Truitt had established a clothing and dry goods store adjoining Harolday's, with a still-limited stock of men's and ladies' wear shipped in from Kansas City. And a nervous little man by the name of Mullens had set up a barbershop next the hotel—lacking a building as yet, he'd simply stretched a tarp to shelter his chair and the cabinet filled with his razors, scissors, and brushes, and was soon at work round the clock serving customers who hadn't known a haircut, or a decent shave, in weeks.

Every new business rated an interview with its proprietor and a story intended for the *Gazette*, while Tanner kept a running score of the things Eden Grove still lacked and sorely needed: A bank, of course—but, no less urgently, a blacksmith, a bootmaker, a dentist, a butcher, a lawyer. . . . And eventually, of course, a school—as sure a sign of maturity as any community could boast.

So far, none of these was as yet on tap; but there was one tent, sprung up like a mushroom on the north side of Union Avenue, that held a considerable interest for Clark Tanner. It stood all alone there, being a whole two blocks north of the town's business center. On the morning following its appearance, he walked over for a look.

Approaching through rank weeds of the vacant lot, he discovered a wagon in process of unloading. There was a haphazard jumble of boxes and crates and odds and ends of furniture, but he could see no one about at the moment. The team stood unharnessed on a tie rope fastened to the wagon's side, with loose hay tossed down for feed.

The tent itself was a large one; erecting it would have been a job for several people. An entrance flap had been fastened back and the sides rolled part way up. As he stepped in, he noted how sounds were muffled by the canvas walls that diffused the sunlight and filled the space with a muted glow. Several benches were stacked along one side. At the rear he made out what he took to be a small cherry-wood pump organ and, near it, a portable lectern of some kind. That, of course, would be the pulpit.

A woman's voice said pleasantly, "Is there something I can do for you?"

Tanner halted as he searched the dim interior and spotted her leaning over an open crate. She had been half hidden by the organ; now she straightened and was watching him, one arm filled with books. "Yes?" she said. "Are you looking for someone?"

"No one in particular," he answered. Coming nearer, he thought he saw her glance waver an instant from his face; he was half expecting that but it turned him cold, all the same, to know it was his limp that had caught her attention. He dreaded the look, both of pity and revulsion, that he had come to identify in the eyes of compassionate strangers before they hastily glanced away. Instead, this one turned to set her books down atop the organ—he saw now they were hymnals—and came at once to meet him, saying, "I'm Katherine Lawless."

He remembered his manners, and his hat was in his hand as he introduced himself.

"Oh—from the newspaper." Her nod was friendly, her smile direct. "James will be sorry he missed you."

"That's all right," he assured her. "There'll be other times. Depending, of course, on how long you expect to be here."

"Oh, we hope to be around for quite a while. Perhaps even permanently. . . . I suppose, because of the tent, you thought we might be revivalists. Not really, Mr. Tanner." And she smiled. She had a nice smile that altered one's first impression that she could be considered plain—it softened the lines of her face and made them interesting. She was a small and tidy woman, younger than he had thought at first glance, and she had a good, trim figure, though the severe shirtwaist and ankle-length skirt did little to show it off. Her hair was black, with a neat center part like a white ruled line, and done in a knot behind her head.

"The tent is a matter of necessity," she explained. "It would be nice, of course, if we had all the money we needed to put up a white church, with a steeple and a bell. But, things don't always work that way. Sometimes you have to start by building a congregation before you can afford the church to hold it. Meanwhile you make do with what you have."

Tanner nodded. "Doesn't sound a lot different, in that respect, from starting a newspaper. . . ."

As they were talking a man had entered at the rear of the tent, carrying a crate that looked almost too heavy for him. He had rounded shoulders on a stringy frame, the ravaged look of a derelict—a reformed drunk, perhaps, saved from the gutter and staying on to help with the heavy work and maybe handle the team and wagon. He put his crate down, gave Tanner an expressionless stare, and went out again.

"I admit I'm a little curious," Clark Tanner said. "I mean, how did you happen to choose a place like Eden Grove? Were you hoping it would live up to its name?"

At that the smile broadened and she actually laughed—a throaty chuckle he found pleasing. "If it did," she pointed out, "there really wouldn't be any need for us, would there? No, James isn't that naïve." She turned quickly serious. "I'm not sure if you know how it is with a preacher, Mr. Tanner. He waits and hopes for a call—the sign to tell him the place where he belongs, where he *is* needed. Sometimes it never comes. But a month ago, after a lot of searching and praying, James became sure for the first time. He had met a man in Kansas City—"

Tanner put in, dryly, "I wonder if that man's name could have been Virgil Beason. . . ."

"You sound skeptical; I can understand. Yes, Mr. Beason struck us both as very much a promoter, smooth spoken and quite glib when it came to selling his town. Even so, the Lord sometimes works through unpromising channels; and Mr. Beason did have an offer for us: this lot, title clear, and a first contribution in cash for the start of a building fund. James didn't see how he could refuse anything that generous."

"For Virgil Beason, I'd say plenty generous! While he was at it, did he offer you credit at the store he owns?"

"Why, yes." She seemed puzzled at the edge she must have heard in his voice. "As a matter of fact, he did. But James and I have always liked to pay as we go."

"You'd be well advised to, in this case." Tanner didn't elaborate. "So, you answered a call to Eden Grove. Now that you're here, what do you think of us?"

She hesitated before trying to answer. "After all we only arrived yesterday," she pointed out. "I don't really know what I expected, but I've never seen a town quite like it. I see places of business, but hardly any homes. And no children at all. Where do people *live?*"

"Wherever they can," he told her. "As a matter of fact, Sam Harolday at the grocery is the only one I know who's actually brought his family with him. But if things work out, in a few weeks you may begin seeing plenty of houses going up, and people coming to live in them—the kind who'd likely be happy to help you build them a church. Right now you're gambling along with the rest of us."

At that, the woman gave him her slow smile. "James might think that an odd way to put it; but then, saving souls has always been a gamble—for the highest stakes of all. So I suppose—how do they say it out here? We're Wisconsin people, ourselves—I suppose we'll just have to give your town a whirl, Mr. Tanner."

Such down-to-earth naturalness warmed him, being far different from what he would have expected from a minister's wife; he found himself responding with a grin. "Fine!" he said. "Right now," he added, "we probably both have work to do. I'll be getting along."

"Do come again—please." She offered her hand and he took it. It was a small hand but, like its owner, it gave an impression of strength. "You will, won't you?"

"I certainly will, Mrs. Lawless," he assured her. "I'm looking forward to meeting your husband."

"My husband?" she echoed. "I've given you the wrong impression. I'm not married, Mr. Tanner. James is my brother; he's a widower, and he and my nephew, Jimmy, are the only family I have. I do what I can to make a home."

"I'm truly glad to hear that!" Clark Tanner exclaimed and then felt his face grow warm, afraid it might have been with too much enthusiasm. He tried to cover up: "I mean—I'm sure they must appreciate all you do for them."

"Thank you," she said quietly, but he thought there was amusement in her look.

She tugged at her hand; realizing he still held it, Tanner hastily let it go. But after that Katherine Lawless merely stood regarding him, and with a sinking feeling he realized she was waiting until he left. That meant he had no choice but to turn and walk away from her. Resigned to it, he set his jaw against the ordeal.

He mumbled something and pulled on his hat.

The distance to the blast of sunlight beyond the entrance flap seemed very great indeed. Tanner started for it, feeling the weight of the woman's look following him as he went dragging that crippled leg down the length of the tent. At the entrance he looked back. Katherine Lawless stood just as he had left her, unmoving. Tanner's mouth tightened and he swung away, blinking in sunlight that was blinding after the dim interior.

Anger and bitterness went with him.

In the year since his crippling, he had come almost to accept what Morgan DuShane's bullet had done. The pain and the physical hampering he could put up with, thankful it hadn't been worse—perhaps fatal; except for an occasional lapse into black melancholy, the determination not to let himself be beaten by such a handicap had served him well.

But courage wasn't proof against moments like this one. He was a young man still, with a young man's normal feelings, and the sign of repugnance in a woman's face was something hard to bear. Yet there had been a naturalness and friendliness about Katherine Lawless that had made him almost, for a moment, forget his problem . . . until the time came when he had to turn his back and leave her there, with no way to disguise the limp that betrayed him for a cripple. . . .

Restless and irritable, Clark Tanner covered the few blocks to Railroad Avenue almost without volition, falling by habit into his customary prowl in search of news. Actually, in his present mood, the affairs of Eden Grove—all the things immediately around him, the raw buildings and the heat shimmer and the snapping of grasshoppers in sun-baked weeds—seemed somehow less real to him than the bitter happenings of a year ago. For, out of that time in Nebraska, a time of heady excitement and determined effort that ended in a single gunshot, the memory of one face always managed to return and haunt him: a face terrifying in the cool, impersonal professionalism of a man who killed for hire, that contained for Clark Tanner all of anguish and humiliation and fear. He knew by this time that it must be forever permanently engraved in his memory.

And now, as he reached the corner of Railroad Avenue, he saw the face again.

He halted in midstride, stunned to alertness; his heart seemed to swell until it clogged his throat. Reason said he must be mistaken, that feverish thought must have played tricks with his vision. But the man who stood talking to Virgil Beason, in the door of the town company office, turned his head and there could be no mistake.

It was! It was Morgan DuShane—lath-lean, clean-shaven, immaculate—in a dark broadcloth coat that did not quite conceal a holstered gun strapped beneath his arm. And across the width of A Street, his eyes met Tanner's and there was sudden recognition in them.

For an interminable instant, their glances locked. Tanner thought DuShane would say something to his companion; but just then Beason turned to open the door and usher him inside, and DuShane went. But as he did his eyes continued to hold Clark Tanner for an instant longer, before the pair of them disappeared into the office.

Unable to move, Tanner stood with the taste of old terror like brass in a mouth gone dry.

# CHAPTER X

Clark Tanner had an old tin trunk, with broken leather straps, in which were stored his personal possessions; here in Eden Grove he had so far unpacked almost nothing except the clothes he wore from day to day. Now, burrowing deep, he found the thing he was looking for—an old revolver, originally made for cap-and-ball but converted to cartridges. Parley Newcome had bought it for him a year ago, after the encounter with Morgan DuShane—apparently, in the fever and delirium of his wound Tanner had ordered him to, out of some half-formed fantasy of revenge. Afterward, when he was once more rational and free of such delusions, the old gun had gone into the trunk and it had stayed there, all during the months of wandering and slow recovery from the bullet that left him permanently crippled.

There was also a box of shells, missing the few that he had once shot off at target practice to test the weapon's accuracy and his own skill; he was dubious of both. Now as he took the gun into his fingers it felt awkward enough, and the palm was damp with cold sweat. He shook his head with a grimace; then straightening, took gun and cartridges and a cleaning rod with him and went out to his worktable in the main room. He laid the gun in front of him and stared at it, waiting for his hands to stop trembling.

With the clumsiness of an unfamiliar task, Clark Tanner used cleaning rod and rag and loaded the weapon with cartridges from the box. Then he let the hammer down on an empty chamber, gingerly, and sat holding the gun while a turmoil of emotions worked in him. A gun was supposed to lend a man confidence; Clark Tanner, sensing the dread potential in each of those little cylinders of brass and powder and lead, felt only his inadequacy to control the power he had in his hand.

As his nerves began to settle, it came to him he was merely giving way to funk. After all, there were no grounds to believe Morgan DuShane's being in town had anything to do with him; the man could have a hundred better reasons. Clark Tanner had been a minor item of business—someone to be eliminated, when he got in the way of interests who were willing to pay DuShane's price. He was probably imagining it, to think the gunman had recognized him or would remember a bread-and-butter job that had occupied him briefly, a year ago, in some faraway and obscure corner of Nebraska.

But if he *did* remember, for Tanner suddenly to start wearing a gun would do very little good, and might simply be the thing to irritate Morgan DuShane and decide him to finish what he had started. Stung by this humiliating truth, Clark Tanner came to his senses. With a shake of his head he pulled open a drawer of the table, dropped the gun and cartridges inside, and violently pushed it shut.

And in that moment he caught a distant mutter of thunder.

It was so long since Tanner had heard such a sound that for an instant he failed to recognize it. He turned quickly to the window; preoccupied as he was, he realized he hadn't been aware of the passing of time, or of a subtle change in the light. He was still not familiar with the weather patterns of these Kansas plains, unable to say whether the clouds would have originated in the distant Rockies, or perhaps come sweeping up from the Gulf. But the sky was solid with them, and a wind had risen and was stripping leaves from the cottonwoods. It brought to him a smell of moisture, of hot dust stirred by the first heavy raindrops. As he watched, lightning flickered on the underbelly of the sky and now a louder rumbling rolled across the Arkansas River bottom.

Even a temporary break in summer heat could mean a welcome relief, though as yet there was no rain. Just now the freight of electricity in the air must surely be adding to the tension that tightened a man's nerves and made his hair seem almost to stand on end. Clark Tanner swore a little as he swung to his feet. He limped back to the water bucket, that was kept filled from one of the town's two wells, and lifted the dipper down from its hook. He was drinking when he heard the street door open; above the dipper's rim, he looked to see who had entered.

Morgan DuShane heeled the door shut and looked at him without speaking and with no readable expression. Neither made any move until, remembering the dipper he was holding, Tanner hastily dropped it into the water pail. He shot a glance toward the table, with its closed drawer, then pulled his stare again to his visitor, bitter in the knowledge that he had been wrong—that for whatever reason, DuShane, after all, still held an interest in him.

Rain began to tap at the roof above their heads, with tentative fingers.

Clark Tanner drew a breath and met the impersonal stare of hazel eyes that, even in the dim light, showed odd flecks of green. "Well," he said tightly. "You've found me. How long did it take?"

One corner of the thin-lipped mouth quirked slightly; DuShane's reply held a raw, scornful edge. "Don't flatter yourself! I haven't been hunting you. Somewhere I did pick up a copy of that thing you're calling a newspaper, and I was amused to see your name and to know you were still around. But it had nothing at all to do with my coming to this town."

Suddenly the rain was coming harder, with a rattling of sleet in it. Rising wind flung it against the building and Tanner had to hurry and slam the window shut above his worktable. This brought him close to the drawer with the loaded gun, and his fingers actually hovered for an instant above the drawer pull. But he had a chill feeling that any sudden move to open it might be the last move he would ever make; he took the hand away.

"I notice you favor your left hip," DuShane commented. "I wonder now, would that be a souvenir? It never occurred to me I could have been so far off the mark—though I did hear that I hadn't killed you, and somebody managed to sneak you out of town. . . ."

Suddenly a year of pain and frustration put an angry tremor in Tanner's voice. "All right, damn you! I didn't really think you'd bother coming all this way from Nebraska, just to make good the shot you bungled. But you *have* followed me to my office. *Why?* Either say what you want with me—or get out and leave me alone!"

The moment the words were out, Clark Tanner found himself astounded at his own temerity; so, it appeared, was DuShane. The green-flecked eyes narrowed. "You don't seem to have learned anything, do you? I was curious to see."

Lightning flared beyond the window; a peal of thunder sounded hard after.

"As for the reason I came to this town," DuShane went on smoothly, "I wanted a look. I've been talking to men from Texas, and I can tell you they really have their eye on this place; there'll be longhorn cattle in those shipping pens before the season's over. Eden Grove is in for a boom, and I plan to ride with it. I've taken out a double lot, south of the tracks; I have the backing and the plans to put up the biggest casino this side of Denver."

"Gambling!" Tanner made no attempt to conceal the note of strong distaste. "Yes, I suppose you'll do well for yourself and your backers." He added, "But I'd still like to know what you want with me. I can hardly believe it's to buy an ad in the *Gazette!*"

"Hardly! No, Tanner, I just wanted to offer you a little advice: You know what happened to you once; it could happen again! I understand you're in thick with a faction that would like to take this town away from the men that started it and set up a government your friends think they could run to suit themselves. After all the trouble they've been to, you can't expect Virgil Beason and his partner to stand still for that—can you?"

"If it's done according to the law," Tanner answered stubbornly, "I suppose they'll have to stand still for it."

"And then there's this operation of mine," DuShane continued as though he hadn't spoken. "Once I've got it set up and going, I'll not enjoy some law badge leaning hard on me, maybe telling me how to run my games."

"In other words, you want a wide-open town."

"It's the Texans who'll want it wide-open," DuShane corrected him. "And they got a right, since it will be the Texas trade, and nothing else, that makes this place." As they talked, DuShane had been looking about at the sparse equipment of the print shop. Now a step took him to the bank of type cases; casually he scooped up a handful of the lead slugs as he went on, too quietly, "You made a nuisance of yourself up there in Nebraska, Tanner; don't do it here! Just have a care what you see fit to print in your paper. You wouldn't like to see all this type scattered in the street like chicken feed—or, the press smashed up so it couldn't be used ever again!"

They faced each other with the warning nakedly open between them—Tanner glaring, DuShane coolly running the leaden slugs from one palm to the other. The wind had diminished; there was a lessening of rain striking the roof. The storm was moving on.

Clark Tanner found his voice and managed to hold it steady. "All right. You made your threat; I'm not apt to forget it."

"See that you don't!" Mission completed, DuShane carelessly tossed the type he was holding back into its case, unconcerned that much of it missed and pattered to the floor instead. He brushed his palms lightly together, adjusted the hang of the coat that concealed the bulge of underarm gun harness; turning to the door, he paused there for a final look at the other man. "Don't make me come back, Tanner," he warned. And with that he was gone into the slackening rain, leaving the door open behind him.

Clark Tanner stood rooted fast, in a state of virtual shock. After a moment he broke free of that, actually shaking his head the way a swimmer does breaking the surface, and moved almost in a trance to his worktable. He still made no move to take out the loaded gun; instead he picked up a paper, looked at it without seeing it, and laid it down again. And Parley Newcome came lunging through the doorway.

Newcome must have been caught by the storm; his clothes were soaked and the thinning gray hair lay plastered to his bare head. His face was ashen, his eyes wild. "Boss!" he cried hoarsely. "Was that who I thought it was, just come out of here?"

Tanner nodded. "It was DuShane."

"But—but—" The old man seemed beyond coherence. "Do you mean, he's tracked you all the way from Nebraska?"

"He says not." Tanner's breathing was almost back to normal now. "And I believe him. I guess it's pure coincidence brought us to the same town. I ran into him on the street, with Virgil Beason; a little later he came around and looked me up."

"He just walked in on you? And then"—Parley Newcome swallowed—"and then walked out again?"

"Without killing me, you mean?" Tanner was actually able to smile a little at the older man's expression. "I still seem to be alive. He just wanted to give me a warning: Mind my own business and not make trouble, or it could be Nebraska all over again."

"Trouble for who? Did he spell it out?"

Tanner nodded bleakly. "He made it clear enough." He told briefly the gist of the exchange with the gunman.

"So it's a gambling hall that brought him here!" Newcome grunted sourly. "I've heard talk of some other things that are fixing to start up, south of the tracks. We don't look out, it could be a regular hell down there when the Texas trade hits; like Abilene, we may have to go out and find us a Wild Bill Hickok!"

He was stripping out of his rain-soaked coat as he went into the back room, to return mopping his face and head on a towel. He had been absorbing what he had learned and now he said darkly, "So the man's lined up with Beason and Colby. There's a real fine combination! . . . Well, and what do *you* figure to do?" he demanded.

"What *can* I do?" Clark Tanner responded. "I'm not running from him again. Where would I go? I've made a start here; if I haven't the guts to stick with it, I can't expect to do any better somewhere else."

Newcome scowled. "I hope you ain't saying this," he suggested with clear reluctance, "because of anything *I* might have let on, about you not having the courage to face up—I've already made my apologies for that. Maybe it's not guts, but just common sense you're shy of. I know, in your place, I'd be scared as hell about now!"

"You think I'm not?" Tanner replied sharply. "But, I won't run! On the other hand, I'm not hunting trouble with DuShane."

"You might not have to hunt too hard. Even if you make a point of never crossing the line, or printing a word he or Beason might not like—I ain't sure Morgan DuShane needs an excuse." Newcome tossed the towel aside, combed damp gray hair in place with his fingers. "You ask me, he's the kind that if he thinks he's got you under his thumb, he might not be able to hold off giving it a twist—just for the fun of it!"

Tanner's mouth set in stubborn lines. "I won't run," he said yet again. Changing the subject, he indicated the compartmented type cases. "I think DuShane spilled some of your type."

That got a rise. "The hell he did!" Parley Newcome exploded. "No sonofabitch messes around my equipment—not even him!" Furious, he hurried to see what damage had been done and to gather up the bits of lead from the floor where DuShane had indifferently scattered them.

By now the sun was out again in full force, and with the window closed the room was quickly like an oven. Tanner shoved it open and looked out on wavers of steam, rising from the briefly dampened earth and from white drifts of hailstones in the hollows. Then, as cooler air began to seep in, he seated himself and dragged a pad of newsprint toward him, to tackle an article that needed writing.

But words and thoughts would not come. He made a number of false starts, angrily scratched them out. Such failure alarmed him. He was no temperamental author—he was a journalist, who took pride in being able to write on any subject, at any moment. Frustrated, he dropped his pencil and wadded the paper and flung it from him, and sat staring at the blank pad.

Yonder, Parley Newcome had found a couple of stories left on the spike for him and was setting them up, his ink-engrained fingers flying as the lines of type built on the stick. Tanner watched in envy, contrasting the fluid movement of the old man's fingers with the tight block that dammed up the words inside his own skull. . . .

There was a sound of voices approaching the open doorway, and now the blast of sunlight there was partly blocked out. Katherine Lawless said, "May we come in?"

Tanner blundered to his feet. The one who followed the girl inside was unmistakably kin—more on the tall side, but with features that showed the same strong bone structure, the same direct look to the brown eyes; his hair, fully as black as hers, was beginning to recede a little. The boy accompanying him, a youngster of perhaps eleven or twelve, was a smaller version of himself. "This is my brother James, Mr. Tanner," the girl said. "And Jimmy."

"Kit tells me I missed you earlier this afternoon," James Lawless said. "I've been wanting to talk to you."

Tanner was favorably impressed. Too many preachers, in these small towns along the prairie frontier, were either tight-lipped fanatics or else crowd-shouters with an eye mainly on the collection plate. This man seemed to be neither. His manner was quiet and his gaze held a hint of sober searching; there was something that suggested he was entirely sincere—and perhaps troubled. Clark Tanner shook hands with him and with the boy, who had some of his father's grave manner. And he introduced Parley Newcome, who only glanced up from the work he was doing to give the visitors a polite nod and a single, searching regard.

By this time Tanner had acquired extra chairs for his office; he brought them out now to offer seats to his guests, but the boy had wandered over to watch Newcome setting type. Kit Lawless said, "Jimmy seems fascinated by anything that has to do with printing and newspapers. It's the first thing he asks about, any new town we come to."

"There are worse ways to make a living," Tanner said briefly, as he took his place behind the worktable; he still felt very uncomfortable with the girl, after that earlier meeting. To the man he said, "Your sister told me you're hoping to build a church here."

Lawless nodded. "You just might be interested to know, I picked up a copy of your paper back in Wichita. I read it carefully; I liked it. To tell you the truth, it was really the deciding factor in bringing me here."

Tanner stared. "You're not serious!"

"Absolutely! Too often, Mr. Tanner, newspapermen give one the impression of being blowhards and braggarts. You on the other hand sounded like a modest man, and an honest one. You resolved some of the doubts I admit I still had after talking to Virgil Beason. I don't know—I just had a feeling I could trust you. And you convinced me I at least wanted to see your town for myself."

"I hope I didn't mislead you any."

"Not likely—believe me. I came into this with my eyes open. I'm well aware it may be an uphill fight, turning Eden Grove into a Christian community." But he smiled as he said it, and it softened the naturally brooding expression. "After all, what other kind of fight is worth while?" To which his sister added brightly, "You see, it's what I meant about having a call, Mr. Tanner. And in this case, you deserve a share of the credit."

All at once Tanner felt his cheeks grow warm with pleasure. "A man does what he can," he said. "If there's any way I can help, I hope you'll let me know."

"Actually," Lawless said, "that's why I'm here. The tent is up and nearly ready. I was wondering about a notice in your paper: Sunday worship at 11 A.M."

"Certainly—though I don't exactly know what kind of attendance you'll get. I doubt there's any real surplus of churchgoers in that crowd of boomers on Railroad Avenue."

Again the quiet smile lightened the somber cast of the other man's features. "I'm afraid there's not exactly a surplus anywhere. . . . What is your charge for the ad, Mr. Tanner?"

"No charge," Tanner said quickly. "I'll be glad to contribute it to the cause."

Lawless thanked him, and then they were on their feet and shaking hands. The boy, who had been keeping close to Parley Newcome, came hurrying over flourishing a strip of newsprint. "Look, Pa! I set up my own name in print. Mr. Newcome showed me how!" He proudly displayed the legend in wetly shining letters: JAMES WARREN LAWLESS, JR.

"The boy has a good eye," Parley Newcome said, joining them. "There's a real knack involved in reading those slugs backwards. Not everybody can pick it up."

As he looked at the youngster's beaming face, and then at Jimmy's aunt, Clark Tanner heard himself making an offer that he knew was less than unselfish. "If he's really that keen about it," he told the preacher, "he's welcome to come around here to the shop any time. There's bound to be ways he can make himself useful—like folding papers and helping deliver them . . . maybe learn to sort type, or lend a hand loading the press. Afraid I can't promise to pay him much, but there's a lot he could pick up about the business."

He had the reward he was fishing for, in the look that warmed Kit Lawless' face and made it, in his eyes, almost beautiful. Jimmy turned breathlessly to his father. "Pa! Could I?"

The latter hesitated only briefly. "I really don't know why not," he said. "We'll think about it." There was more handshaking, then, and Clark Tanner kept the woman's hand for seconds longer than was really necessary. Afterwards he walked to the door with the three of them and watched them move off through the steaming sunlight, holding to the memory of Kit Lawless' touch and the last smile she threw him.

It had been—he could almost swear it—the friendly smile of a woman who seemed not even aware that he was a cripple. . . .

# CHAPTER XI

Lucy Harolday lifted the lid from the firebox, to drop in the last piece of cottonwood branch. She moved pans around on the stove, adjusted the draft as the tinder-dry fuel broke into roaring flame, and after that stood a moment listening, with a frown, to the sound of an ax at work behind the store. Knowing her husband well, she had put off as long as she could mentioning the empty woodbox; his sole answer had been a grunt and a peevish shrug as he snatched up the ax and went stalking outside, Jeanie toddling after to watch.

It didn't do to blame him too much; chopping firewood was a task Sam hated above all others. Besides, the few words he'd spoken earlier suggested that Mr. Beason must have had him on the carpet, over some matter in connection with running the store. It gave her no pleasure to upset him even further. Lucy would gladly have filled the box herself, but she had tried before this and the ax was just too heavy for her to manage. Besides— and her frown tightened—that was his own dinner warming on the stove. Was it fair he should act as though he were being abused because she dared to remind him of a chore?

Sighing, she set the damper again and then stepped up to the cupboard to take down dishes for the table. As she was reaching for them she became aware of a sound in the front part of the building; a customer's wants came first, always. Lucy Harolday left her work and went to see what was needed.

The curtain whispered into place behind her as she halted, staring at a sight she had never seen before: someone on the wrong side of the service counter, where no customer had any business to be. He had heard. He whipped his head around, and she knew him—she looked at light yellow hair, and a sunburned face, and then her glance moved quickly down the lanky, overalled length of the boy and discovered the reason he hadn't made more noise than he did: His feet were bare.

Blue eyes stared back at her in a face gone slack with fear. It was Lucy who broke the silence, exclaiming, "What do you want?"

She got no answer. The boy was poised in a half crouch, her look pinning him. But now she saw what he was holding—the store's cashbox, a cigar box really, that was kept on a shelf below the counter. The breath caught in her throat. "Oh no!" she cried in protest. "No! You mustn't. . . ."

He seemed unable to move or to speak. Lucy took a tentative step toward him, a hand going out—she hardly knew whether in pleading, or to try and wrest the box from him. At once he drew away, clutching it more tightly, and she hesitated. "Put the money back," she told him, trying to speak slowly and clearly. "You don't really want to do this!"

They were interrupted, then. A heavy footstep sounded; the curtain was jerked aside and Sam Harolday appeared in the opening, a load of kindling stacked in the bend of one arm. He must have heard his wife's voice; he looked at her first, and then at the boy, and she saw his face darken in understanding. The wood dropped with a clatter. "You!" he shouted harshly. "What do you think you're up to?"

That seemed to cut through whatever numbness held the tow-headed youngster in its grip. Instantly he wheeled, darted around the end of the counter, and was off at a padding run, still grasping the box. Harolday yelled as he started after him, then instead paused to grope for something beneath the counter. Though Lucy quickly guessed what he was after, she gave a horrified gasp as she actually saw the gleam of the revolver. "Don't—don't shoot!" She caught at her husband's arm.

Impatiently Harolday shook her off, pain sending weakness through her as the back of his hand struck hard against a breast. Seeing the fugitive about to escape, Harolday swore and lunged in pursuit. Lucy got her breath, to cry out in anguish, "Sam! Sam, he's only a *boy!*"

The words had no effect and next moment she set her foot on one of the treacherous lengths of cottonwood. Hampered by clinging skirts she fell heavily; she was almost sobbing as she pushed hurriedly to her feet again. Her husband had gained the doorway and stood framed there, in profile as he leveled the gun at arm's length, taking deliberate aim. Lucy, reaching his side, had a glimpse of the lad sprinting away along the line of building fronts, while men stopped to turn and stare after him. It was an easy target that Harolday could scarcely miss.

But at the last instant—perhaps, after all, his wife's shocked cries had registered—Sam Harolday tilted the gun barrel a fraction and sent his bullet over the fugitive's head, at the same time yelling, "Stop, thief! *Stop him!*"

The boy veered wildly as the shot sounded, and an instant later he had ducked into the space between a pair of buildings and vanished. Lucy Harolday felt herself go limp. She clutched the frame of the door to steady herself; trying to form the words to thank her husband, she was quelled by the acid look he gave her— a look that said, *You see, now, what you made me do!* Then he was off in pursuit, the smoking gun in his fist.

And Railroad Avenue began to come alive to the excitement of a man hunt in progress.

Hans Burkhalter lay bellied down in the cramped space under Booker's furniture store and listened to them search for him. In contrast with the day's heat, the shadowed dirt here was cold and almost damp, so that fear and chilling sweat combined to send long, racking shivers running through him; he had to clamp his jaws to keep his teeth from chattering. He still had the cashbox, clutched against him with its hard corner digging into a rib. Running with it, he had heard a metallic jingle of coins and felt paper money shifting; but since diving into his hole he had not even thought to look inside the box or try to see, in the dim light, how much he had got away with. He was too frightened—too sick at heart.

He no longer, consciously, even thought about the money.

It was unmanly to cry; he never had since he was seven, not even when his father whipped him—he would bite his lip, first, till the blood ran. But at this moment terror and despair came near to overwhelming him, and the enormity of what he had done. Only his family's desperate need could have driven him to it—the crops dying in this unfamiliar ground, his parents depriving themselves so the younger children shouldn't know what it was to go to bed hungry.

But the pinched and haunted look of his mother, and Emil Burkhalter's stolid and unvoiced bitterness, had been the goad that finally sent him, on foot, the half-dozen miles into town—not really knowing what he intended but somehow obsessed with that scene when he'd heard his father accuse the storekeeper of cheating him. The plan must have been half formed already in the back of his mind; but it struck him almost as a revelation, the moment when he looked in and saw the store empty and unattended, and reasoned there must be money there, perhaps behind the counter.

He hadn't stopped to think how he would explain the money to his father. Perhaps, unlikely as it was, he'd supposed Emil Burkhalter was desperate enough to forget his principles for once and not ask too many questions. . . .

Now he lay trembling with his face in the dirt and listened to voices yelling back and forth in the streets and alleyways, the tramp of man hunters past his hiding place. He wondered when someone was going to notice this dark opening beneath the building foundation, and simply reach in and drag him out.

Dimly, though, he sensed it was only the excitement of the chase that pushed these men—they could hardly care that much about getting back Sam Harolday's cashbox. So the longer he stayed where he was, the better the chance they would grow tired of the whole business and turn to something else. Lie low until dark, he told himself—a long time, admittedly, because these summer twilights seemed to last forever. But with luck he should be able then to escape from here and find his way clear out of town without anyone seeing him. At this comforting thought, the wrenching shudders through his body began to ease their severity.

And then there were more footsteps, drawing nearer, and the voices of a pair of men came louder. They halted abruptly, almost on top of his hiding place. Someone said, quite distinctly, "Now, what do you suppose would be under there?"

Every muscle of the fugitive's body locked in tension as the second voice said, "The kid, you think?"

"Well, he's got to be someplace."

"Don't hardly seem room enough. . . ." Nevertheless shoe leather scraped and suddenly the dim light of the opening was completely shut out. Hans tried to flatten himself into the dirt— not daring to look, aware that the two men had knelt and were peering into the hole but blocking it with their bodies. They were close enough he could hear them breathe.

The first said, "Too dark—I can't see a thing."

"Hell! Nothing bigger than a pack rat could hide in there. Let's go!"

"Not yet. You got matches?" The dubious one grunted a negative, but his companion remained insistent. "Stay here and keep an eye open. I'll fetch a lantern."

"Waste of time!" the second man grumbled, as the shadows withdrew. After that someone hurried away, but Hans knew the other was still out there; a groan of agony and terror almost broke through his hard-clenched jaws.

There was no other way out of this hole—the boy had checked that already. It meant he was trapped, with no choice but simply to lie and wait for them to bring their lantern and thrust it in his face, and find him there. And what would Emil Burkhalter do when he learned his son had been captured and branded a thief?

Suddenly that was the very worst thought of all. . . .

Helpless, he felt the slow crawling of the minutes and the slow tightening of his gut. But the one who had been left to guard his hole was feeling the waiting, too; it was he, after all, who had objected to spending time on this in the first place. The boy heard him moving back and forth out there like a man growing impatient. Suddenly he said, quite distinctly, "Aw, the hell with it!" And next moment he was walking, deliberately and hurriedly, away.

Even when he had gone, young Burkhalter could not at first believe it. Then the fact struck home, and with it the realization: This was a reprieve—but he might not have it long.

After so long in one position, cramped limbs threatened not to obey. Scrabbling and scrambling, he came clawing out of the hole like a badger and got his legs under him, though the need for haste turned his knees unsteady, and he thought for an instant they might buckle. There was a deep flooding of relief when he turned the corner at the rear of the furniture store and hauled up a moment, somehow still clutching the cigar box, breath sawing brokenly in his throat as he pressed a hand against the rough clapboards to steady himself.

Quiet seemed to have settled over the town of Eden Grove; he could hear no more shouting, nothing to indicate the man hunt was still going on. Maybe the two who nearly trapped him under Booker's furniture store had been the last of the searchers, and now with any luck he had a chance of getting away.

Beyond the unmarked alley, backed up to it and facing the next street north, a new building was under construction—only a raised flooring, as yet, and a forest of partition timbers in clean yellow pine. The ground about was littered with chips and sawdust, and he saw a couple of stacks of boards. No one seemed to be working the site just then, and breaking free of where he stood he hurried forward and took cover again behind one of the lumber piles, while he filled his lungs with the pungent scent of pine and scouted his next step.

He wouldn't run, he told himself; that was the surest way of drawing attention. He would ease up from his hiding place and walk away, acting natural—cut across the building site to the street beyond and keep walking. The main thing was not to lose his head, or in any way act suspicious. . . .

He straightened to his feet and willed himself to move into the open.

He had taken a couple of steps when he saw, from the tail of his eye, the man who stood at one corner of the building skeleton. The sight halted him in his tracks and whipped his head around to stare. Spare, erect, in a dark broadcloth coat despite the summer heat, the man regarded him with odd-looking hazel eyes. The thin lips barely moved as he spoke. "Going somewhere with that box, kid?"

The boy had all but forgotten he still had it. His mind was suddenly empty of thought, and at any rate words could not have forced their way past the lump of despair. Helpless, he stood and watched the man put a hand into the gap of his coat front. But when the hand reappeared, sight of the gun it held jarred young Burkhalter into convulsive movement.

He lost his head and flung the box straight at the man with the gun. The lid sprang open, strewing coins and greenbacks; at the same moment the boy was starting a wild and hopeless dash for the building's nearest corner. It seemed an enormous distance.

The gun cracked, flatly. He felt a blow that threw him violently offstride, and filled him with numbness even as he fought to keep his legs working.

He never felt the second bullet, or knew when he stumbled and went down in a loose sprawl, headlong on the hardpacked dirt.

In deepening night, with a last line of light showing along the flat horizon, there was not much to see of the homestead. Lamp glow showed yellow in the doorway and window of the sod house. A second crude structure, fashioned, like the house, of squares of turf laboriously chopped out and piled up in a semblance of walls, would serve the purpose of a barn and a storeroom for such tools as the owner possessed for working this tough Kansas earth. Halting the buggy John Riggs had insisted on lending him for his errand, Tanner looked about the silent farmyard, with the reins in his hands and the horse stomping, seeing now the well, with a sweep, on which the farm depended for water, and the old wagon parked nearby.

A voice called, "Yah?" It was a challenge; a man walked out of the shadows, into the glow of the carriage lamps. Emil Burkhalter stood with his big hands hanging at his sides, his head bare, suspicion in the probing look with which he tried to make out the faces of the men beneath the buggy top. Clark Tanner leaned forward, bringing his own into the light.

"Mr. Burkhalter?" he said. "My name's Tanner. I don't know if you'll remember me. I saw you at Harolday's store, a couple of weeks ago."

The German's yellow hair looked like a tangle of white straw above his craggy, unsmiling features. He looked at Tanner and he nodded shortly, once. "I remember."

"This is the Reverend Lawless." Tanner indicated the one beside him. "He's the new preacher, just come to Eden Grove within the past week. He—" Tanner hesitated; in the face of the homesteader's unyielding expression, this was proving harder even than he had anticipated. "The two of us volunteered to drive out this evening, Mr. Burkhalter. It's about your son. . . ."

"I have three sons," the German said. "The two young ones are inside. If it's Hans you want, he isn't here."

"We know that."

For the first time, the man showed a definite reaction other than hostile suspicion. His head lifted; the glow of the lamp struck directly across his eyes and revealed them as a startling, pale blue. "My boy is in trouble? You come to tell me that?"

Tanner drew a breath. "We came to tell you he's been shot, Mr. Burkhalter. I'm very sorry."

"He's dead." It was a statement, not a question.

"I'm sorry," Clark Tanner repeated, and it sounded lame enough to him. Resolutely he continued: "You'll have to know the rest of it, sooner or later. He tried to rob Harolday."

"A lie!"

Lawless spoke for the first time. "I'm afraid it's the truth. He took the cashbox. A dozen men saw him running with it, and he had it when he was killed. I sincerely wish there was some room for doubt."

A silence. Then: "If you're a preacher, I guess I have to take your word. . . . Who shot him?"

Clark Tanner could see no point in holding that back, either. "A man by the name of DuShane," he answered. "There was something of a man hunt. DuShane just happened to be the one who caught up with him."

"My Hans had a gun? Where did he get a gun?"

"He didn't."

"Then why was he shot?"

Tanner thought of the two wounds he had seen, either one of which would have killed—one in the right side, the other between the shoulders after the force of the first bullet spun the boy's slight shape around. Still, it would serve no good purpose to explain about Morgan DuShane; he said only, "Who knows how things like that happen?"

"Where is my son?" the man wanted to know.

"They took him to Dr. Riggs. The doctor tried his best, but it was already too late. He's holding the body, for now."

The horse moved restlessly and Tanner settled it with the reins. James Lawless spoke again into the silence. "I know there's very little anyone can do, Mr. Burkhalter, but I came to be of any help

I could. I'll break the news to the mother, if you would want me to."

Burkhalter moved his massive shoulders, as though to break free of a weight that lay on them. "No, I tell her," he said firmly, and abruptly turned away. After a few steps he seemed to remember his visitors, still seated in the buggy. He halted long enough to look back and fling a crude invitation: "You come." It was more like an order, and he left them with it as he strode stolidly on to the house. Tanner and Lawless exchanged a look; with a shrug, Tanner flicked the reins.

When they entered the house, removing their hats and ducking the low entrance doorway, they saw how this family lived. There appeared to be two rooms, a curtained doorway between. The interior was something like a cave and surprisingly neat, the dirt walls smoothed off with the bit of a spade and muslin spread under the ceiling—a precaution against loose dirt and spiders. The trestle table and the packing-case cupboards had been hand-fashioned; a widemouthed hearth served for both cooking and for heat.

The three youngest children were already at the table—Tanner saw a platter containing a few meager pieces of what he took to be rabbit, a bowl of greens of some kind. A pitcher contained milk; the Burkhalters appeared to own a cow.

Emil Burkhalter stood facing his wife, and apparently he had already broken the news; her face was drained of color, and she had both hands pressed against her mouth. The children looked on, wide-eyed.

A single sob broke from the woman, muffled behind her fingers. Emil Burkhalter's face, by lamplight, looked old and drawn. He said brokenly, "I can't understand! I never raise our son to steal."

"He was no thief," his wife said, and let her hands fall heavily. "He only did it because he wanted to try and help. I know!"

"To steal is wrong," the German said doggedly. "Is wrong!"

"Would it help to pray?" James Lawless suggested gently.

Burkhalter nodded without raising his eyes; and there in the stillness of the soddy, with the flames of the cookfire snapping on the hearth, the preacher spoke quiet words that, to Clark Tanner, seemed just the right ones for this moment and place. Afterward he couldn't have repeated the words exactly, but they'd been enough to convince him this earnest-eyed young fellow was no Bible-thumper. Not particularly religious himself, Tanner could see that Eden Grove had acquired a good man in its first parson, and he was pleased.

"I got no manners!" Emil Burkhalter exclaimed almost before the last words of the prayer were spoken. "You will sit to table with us, of course."

Looking at the scant meal, Tanner made hurried excuses. "We have to get back. We only wanted to give you the news—and also to find out what you want done. There's a place on the bluff above the town that's being set aside for a cemetery—though nobody expected to see it put to use, quite this soon! If you like—"

"No!" Burkhalter replied flatly. "Not among strangers. This is his home. We bring him and we bury him here."

"Whatever you say."

But the woman spoke then, quietly but with determination. "We will bury him in town," she told her husband. "If we lose this farm the way we lost the others, then there'll be no one. In the cemetery, he'll have folks around him—even if they're strangers; that is better."

The German lifted his head sharply as though to protest, but he saw the look on his wife's face and he nodded. "All right. In town."

"Tomorrow at noon?" Lawless suggested. "I'll be glad to make all the arrangements. We'll send someone out for you and your family."

Burkhalter made a gesture with one hand. "No need. We will be there."

It left nothing more to say. A few murmured good nights, and the pair from town took their departure. In the door, Tanner looked back for a moment at the dingy, lamplit room and at these people, crushed by this thing that had happened. He saw the mother trying to comfort her little girl who was weeping now—even she realized, at last, that her big brother Hans was dead.

He could only turn his back on the scene and follow Lawless to the waiting buggy.

# CHAPTER XII

Tanner, with Parley Newcome at his elbow, found himself wondering on just what impulse some of the dozen or so people gathered about young Hans Burkhalter's grave were doing there. Simple curiosity, he supposed, in the case of the few rootless boomers who for lack of better to do had trudged up the trail through the grove, to this point overlooking the Arkansas bottom. Merv Booker, the furniture dealer, might have come to see the first pine coffin from his stock lowered into the sandy soil. Virgil Beason could be here out of some dim sense of obligation—or perhaps to see Eden Grove's cemetery formally inaugurated.

Beason had brought the Haroldays with him, in his two-seated rig. Sam Harolday looked stern and handsome, in a well-cut town suit and polished button shoes and bowler hat; but the July afternoon had the man sweating and uncomfortable. He would probably rather be almost anywhere else; Tanner had an idea his wife must have put some kind of pressure on him.

Kit Lawless was staying close to Mrs. Burkhalter, ready to be of help if she should be needed; they, and Lucy Harolday, were the only women present. Aside from the Burkhalter children and the Haroldays' little girl and Jimmy Lawless, the rest of the group were men. Tanner nodded a solemn greeting to Phil Steadman and Doc Riggs, who had come up together. Waiting to one side, keeping out of the way as the ceremony began, the Lawlesses' handy man—the whiskey-broken reprobate whom Tanner had never heard called anything more than "Luther"—leaned on his shovel and waited for the time to refill the hole he had dug.

Not unnaturally, there was no trace of Morgan DuShane.

That brief rain of a few days ago had been absorbed and forgotten, and the mound of dirt from the grave was powder dry; the constant plains' wind plucked it and carried it away in streamers.

When Lawless began to speak and the men removed their hats, the hot wind whipped at their hair, as it tugged sharply at their coats and the skirts of the women. Lawless had to raise his voice to be heard above it.

He kept the ceremony brief and simple and direct, which Tanner found entirely fitting. He placed no blame. He spoke of the tragic shortness of the life they were consigning to the grave, but other than that he said only that Hans Burkhalter had been very young and devoted to his people, and it was for the Lord to judge whether he had paid for any mistake he might have committed. Lawless read a few words from the black leather Bible, said a prayer, and it was over.

Kit Lawless stepped forward to lay a sprig of prairie flowers on the cheap pine box, and then it was lowered into the hole on ropes and the ropes freed and whisked away, and the group began to disperse. The dead boy's mother was pale as ashes under the sun-beaten weathering of her features. Tanner watched her narrowly, but she moved steadily enough, with head erect, as she herded her brood of children toward the old wagon in which they had made the journey in from their homestead.

Virgil Beason passed Tanner, and the latter heard his carrying voice: "A dandy location for a cemetery—an excellent view. We'll need to see about putting up a fence and a gate with a proper sign over it. . . ." Looking again at the solitary grave, Tanner found himself remembering with irony how Mrs. Burkhalter had insisted the burial be held here instead of at the farm: *In the cemetery he'll have folks around him.* . . . And now everyone was going away and leaving him here, all alone.

Who would be the first to join him in this particular "fine and private place"—and how soon?

At that moment Tanner heard, distantly, a sound that brought his head up with a start. He might have thought it a vagary of the restless wind, but he instantly knew otherwise. He turned to the low bluff, that gave him a view over the roofs and streets of Eden Grove and the river like a streak of quicksilver under the high sun. As he stood listening, the sound was repeated, far off somewhere down the valley. There was a footstep beside him, and Kit Lawless asked, a little breathlessly, "Did you hear it, too? Like the whistle of a locomotive."

Tanner nodded. "That's what it was. A work engine, hauling up ties and steel—and close enough, for the first time, that we can hear it. . . ."

The bridge crew had done its trestle building in short order and moved on; now, from this point, they could see a smear of dust raised by mule-drawn fresno scrapers and pick-and-shovel gangs. Once they had prepared the right-of-way, the final laying of track would bring the rails at last into Eden Grove—a matter of days, now, according to the Santa Fe's own timetable.

Suddenly, despite the hot slant of the sun, he felt a touch of chill. He thought again of the question he'd asked himself just now, as he stood beside Hans Burkhalter's lonely grave. *How soon?* he had wondered; and it was as though the echo of that distant work engine had given him the answer. Something that had been unsettled in his mind turned over and dropped into place. A doubt was resolved.

This was Thursday: press day. With the deadline nearing, he had been in a real turmoil to know just how much he could afford to say in his columns about the circumstances of the boy's death. Now he knew that it held far wider implications that could not be ignored. Like it or not there was, suddenly, only one thing for him to do.

He turned and looked at the girl and saw her staring at him; he wondered if his own expression told her of the hard decision he had just arrived at.

Sam Harolday watched the Burkhalters prepare to leave the graveyard, moving about their wagon like people turned wooden with grief. He could feel the quiet weight of his wife's regard and knew that she was not going to let him off. He let her see his displeasure, both in his scowl and the shrug of resignation with which he settled the coat in place. But his stride was firm enough as he started over there, Lucy and Jeanie following him hand in hand.

The Burkhalter children were already in their places in the wagon bed; the farmer was about to give his wife a hand-up when he stiffened, his expression gone stony at sight of Harolday. The latter halted and they stood there in the weeds, eyeing each other, neither speaking.

Sam Harolday drew a breath. "Burkhalter," he said, "this has been a dreadful tragedy. I don't suppose it does any real good to say how much I regret it."

For a long interval he got no reply, saw no change in the hard cast of that stolid German face. Barely nodding, then, the man said, "All right."

Determinedly, Harolday continued. "I didn't really know your son. In spite of what happened, I'm sure he was a decent lad, well brought up. Everything else aside, I can imagine the extra hardship it's going to mean for you, working that farm with one fewer pair of hands."

The heavy shoulders lifted. "We get along."

"Of course—of course. All the same . . ." Receiving no help, Harolday mentally backed up and plunged on a different course. "I've been discussing your account with the owners of the store. I've assured them you're a thoroughly honest man—one customer, at least, that can be counted on to meet his obligations if it's any way possible. I convinced them it would be in their own interest to help see you make a go of it."

At something he said, the other man drew back sharply. The blue eyes fairly glittered. "You tell them I take charity?"

"Certainly not!" Harolday was sweating even more. "But I did make an arrangement with them. If you'll come in—today if you like—you're welcome to load up whatever supplies you happen to need. And I can promise there'll be no further interest charges. Frankly, we want your business—enough, that we're willing to make an exception for you."

He thought for a moment he was going to get no answer at all. But finally Emil Burkhalter said, "Very well. I come in." And after that—grudgingly, as though it went hard against the grain—a brief: "Thank you. . . ."

Sam Harolday nodded; the matter was settled.

He turned to his wife. Lucy had been speaking quietly to Burkhalter's wife, while Jeanie and the children in the wagon solemnly regarded one another. Harolday heard his wife say, "Your little girl and mine are nearly the same age. Maybe they'd enjoy playing together sometime."

"Maybe," the farm woman said dubiously. "We don't get in town often. But—we see."

The thing broke up then, Harolday turning his family in the direction of the buggy where Virgil Beason impatiently awaited them. They went in silence; but, just for a moment, Lucy Harolday laid a hand on her husband's wrist and let it rest there—a gesture of appreciation and approval, wholly unexpected and much too quickly ended.

Long before Tanner arrived at the print shop, that injured hip was aching dully from the haste of his tramp off the bluff above town; and yet as he sat at his worktable, scrawling words that seemed to leap into his mind without the necessity of thinking, it suddenly occurred to him the leg hadn't hurt him nearly so much of late. He half suspected this might be because Kit Lawless didn't seem to notice he was a cripple, or to bc bothered by it if she did. His hand paused in the middle of a word as he let that thought have its way with him, and wondered at it.

He thought she genuinely liked him, almost as much as he found himself liking her after this short time, and his lameness didn't signify. He almost dared to believe he could accept that at its face value. . . .

The writing done, the last correction made, he was looking over what he had penned when Parley Newcome came in. "You're late," he said, without thinking, before he looked up and read the truth in the old man's face.

"I stopped in at Cotton's and had me a drink," Newcome said defiantly. "I needed it—that business up on the hill had me depressed." But then, under Tanner's look, he added in a gruff voice, "Just one drink, though. I ain't completely a fool; I know we got a paper to put to bed."

"All right," Tanner said, dismissing the matter of the drink—though a faint blurring of Newcome's speech, and the slightly off-focus stare, raised doubts as to whether he was being strictly truthful about the limit he'd set himself. But, drunk or sober, Parley Newcome could handle a composing stick with any man; Tanner handed him the new copy. "I want this on the front page. We can juggle what's already set up, to make room; I don't care what we have to jerk. This goes in."

Newcome was a quick and agile compositor, but a slow reader. Tanner watched his eyes as they tracked down the scrawled lines, his lips silently forming the words. Suddenly the eyes widened and he lifted his head to stare at his employer. He stammered a little. "You real sure about this?"

"Do you mean, am I going to change my mind? I can't very well, can I—once it's printed and on the street?"

The older man met his employer's look squarely. He said bluntly, "I mean, this don't sound much like anything you been saying. What makes the difference now?"

It was a fair question. Tanner answered him soberly. "After the services today, up on the bluff, there was an entirely new sound: an engine whistle, somewhere off down the valley."

"You heard that too, did you?" Newcome wagged his grizzled head. "The rails are getting closer."

"Until that moment, I don't think it had dawned on me just *how* close—what's going to happen to this town, and how little time we have."

"All the same"—Parley Newcome tapped the page he held, with an ink-grimed finger—"print this and you're going to bust a bombshell!"

The other man lifted a shoulder. "I suppose. Just go ahead and set it up, and let's see how it looks." And when the other man still hesitated: "You don't mind too much, do you?"

They shared a look, and sudden understanding passed between them. The sour mood that had clung to Parley Newcome, like the smell of the booze he brought into the office with him, visibly lifted. His head came up and a grin bunched his whiskered cheeks. "Hell!" he said, all at once in high good humor. "It'll be a pleasure. . . ."

Incredibly soon he was back, the story set up and the wet ink still glistening on the galley proof he had pulled on it. He laid the strip of newsprint in front of Tanner without a word; the latter read it through briefly for errors that he failed to find—but with a growing weight settling in his middle as he saw, in cold type, the enormity of what he had dashed off in the white heat of inspiration:

### THE NEED FOR ORDER

Yesterday we had our first killing in Eden Grove. How many more will follow?

A fifteen-year-old boy was shot to death, allegedly in the commission of a robbery—he is reported to have had the money with him. As a thief and a fugitive, he was of course fair game. But he was also unarmed—and there were better ways to serve justice than by deliberately shooting him down, in cold blood.

Less than two weeks from now, we are told, the railroad will reach this city. It is the hope of everyone, naturally, that this will bring us the lucrative business in Texas cattle; at the same time it is only prudent that we profit by the example of Abilene, Ellsworth, and other towns which have already enjoyed the Texas trade, but have also experienced less desirable side effects.

It now seems to us there can be but one solution: Eden Grove needs law, and needs it soon, with responsible officials to enforce justice and not leave it to the whim of any bystander with a gun. This can only be had through government, for which we need organization under legal statute. We can achieve this through petition of the proper law court, and steps should be taken at once.

Our time is running out.

Parley Newcome, watching his employer's face closely, said, "All right?"

Tanner nodded. "Print it." He showed some page proofs he had been marking. "Move these two stories back to the second page to make room, and kill the piece about Booker's new shipment of furniture. No—better yet, save that. We can use it in the next issue. If there *is* a next issue," he added dryly.

"I guess you realize, then, what you're doing," Newcome said. "Beason's not going to take it kindly, you throwing the *Gazette* behind the move for organization. And DuShane . . . my God! You're all but calling him a murderer!"

"Damn it, he *is* a murderer! Thief or not, there was no excuse to kill that boy. He shot young Burkhalter twice—almost as though he was doing it for pleasure!"

Newcome predicted sourly, "It's nothing to the pleasure he'll get out of putting a bullet in *you*, once he reads this! And don't count on his aim being off—not a second time. You used up all *that* kind of luck you had, in Nebraska!"

Clark Tanner met his look for a silent moment. Deliberately, then, he opened the drawer of his worktable; he heard the older man's exclamation when he took out the ancient six-shooter and laid it in front of him.

"Hell! We both know you're no good with a gun."

"I guess I can be if I have to."

"Not against Morg DuShane! You put that thing on and you're dead; it's all the excuse he'll need to kill you. . . ." Suddenly the older man thrust out a shaking hand. "I got a better suggestion. Let *me* have that, boss."

Tanner stared. "You? This had got nothing to do with you."

"All the more reason DuShane won't be expecting it. He won't even be looking my direction. He sees me, he won't know I'm there till it's too late."

"No!" Sternly shaking his head, Clark Tanner placed a hand on the gun to forestall him. "You aren't going to fight my battles! I already owe you too much. Your only job now is to get those forms set up and start that press to working. And I want to see you doing it!"

They eyed each other almost in hostility; it was Parley Newcome who backed away. His shoulders lifted; he expelled his breath in an exasperated gust and swung about to stalk off angrily toward the waiting press.

Remembering something, he halted long enough to say gruffly, "I told Jimmy Lawless he could come in this evening and watch the run. Any objections?"

He was curt and belligerent, and Tanner held on to his temper with some difficulty as he answered, "Why should there be? You know I already told him he was welcome."

"I won't let him get in the way," Newcome went on stubbornly, as though he hadn't been answered. "The kid's wild to learn anything he can about a print shop and putting a newspaper together. Though sometimes," he added sourly, as he turned away again, "I wonder why the hell I'd want to encourage anybody getting into *this* damn business!"

Tanner let that go without comment.

So the afternoon passed. With his part of the work finished and nothing more to contribute toward putting out the paper, Tanner turned to the chore of fixing a meal. Once, hearing voices, he looked in from the back room to see that Jimmy Lawless had arrived; he tried not to allow himself a pang of disappointment because the boy's aunt Katherine hadn't come with him—which would be foolish, since there had been no reason to expect her. Still, almost unconsciously, he had hoped. When beans and coffee were heated he ate alone, Parley Newcome saying he was too busy just then and Jimmy having already had his supper. Afterward, Tanner stepped out to make a final tour of the town.

Since he had decided he was going to have to get used to carrying the gun, he shoved it behind the waistband of his trousers in a way so the hang of the coat front concealed it. A spray of lemon light still stained the sky in the west, but stars were out and were echoed by the lights of the town, the latter making him realize how much things had changed in the few short weeks he'd been here.

Construction was starting to spill north, back from the original line of the buildings on Railroad Avenue; the number of buildings finished and under construction was on its way to doubling. He saw the bulking shape of the Lawless tent, with a faint glow of lamplight behind the canvas, and that made him think of the solitary grave on the bluff like a raw wound in the earth. He couldn't help wondering if Hans Burkhalter was lonely tonight up there by himself.

The town seemed normally quiet, except for the usual noise from Railroad Avenue. He made his rounds looking for news but hearing none. He saw nothing at all of Morgan DuShane. In Cotton's saloon there was some talk of the killing; otherwise it was the ordinary run of speculation and rumor. In the glassless window of the new railroad depot a lamp glowed—the bridge crew had left a watchman there, against the risk of drunks and sabotage. Tanner had already talked to him, got what little of story value the man had to give.

A newsman had a way of sensing news or the absence of it. Tonight the town had nothing for him; he might as well go home and help put the paper to bed. Tomorrow, if he was any judge, the storm should break.

# CHAPTER XIII

Parley Newcome, thinning hair awry, came out into the print shop squinting at morning light and scratching his narrow chest through the gap in his underwear. He found Tanner drinking coffee and looking over a copy of the *Gazette*, from the neat stack on the worktable; he said, "Well, how does it look by daylight?"

Tanner nodded. "It looks fine. You did a good job, as usual."

Newcome dismissed that with a shrug. "The old press held up for once—never even threatened to break down on me. And the boy was a lot of help, too. . . . I was just wondering if you had any second thoughts about that piece you wrote, now that you see it in print."

Tanner gave him a wry look. "Plenty of second thoughts— maybe some thirds and fourths. But, it will have to stand."

"Too late to change your mind," the older man agreed, "even if you wanted to. I told you about Phil Steadman dropping in last evening while we were running them off; you knew he'd be tickled pink, after the way he's been fighting for a petition to get the town organized. He had several copies with him when he left—so, I'd guess by this time everybody around is going to know what you wrote, including Beason. And Morg DuShane," he added.

Tanner considered that, but shook his head. "Makes no great difference. They'll have to know."

"The Lawless youngster said he'd be coming back this morning. He wants to help deliver papers, and I figured it would be all right. He can take them to the hotel and the stores; I'll handle the places on Railroad Avenue where a twelve-year-old oughtn't to go. I'm looking forward to seeing Beason's face when he reads that editorial."

Giving him a shrewd look his boss said, "I see what you're up to. But I won't let you take the heat for me. The trouble is between me and Beason; I'll face him myself."

Parley Newcome shrugged inside his sweated underwear. "I figured as much. I was just suggesting. . . ."

"Sure." Tanner laid the paper down and felt of the stubble on his jaws. "While I'm shaving," he suggested, "how about bundling up those overruns and getting them ready? I'll take them over to Beason first thing, and have it done with."

"I ain't sure he's going to want any extra thousand copies of *this* paper."

"He ordered them. He's getting them!"

Tanner caught the older man's stare—as much as to say, *This is really you talking?* But Parley Newcome let it go.

Later, Clark Tanner wiped his razor dry and tossed the soapy water out the back door. Buttoning his shirt, he re-entered the shop to find Newcome talking with Doc Riggs and Phil Steadman. He sensed at once an undercurrent of excitement and accomplishment. Without comment, Steadman handed him a sheet of legal paper with a heading penned in the hotelkeeper's neat, copperplate handwriting. It was addressed to the probate judge at Hutchinson, petitioning on behalf of the signators that Eden Grove, Kansas, be officially organized as a city of the third class.

Watching him read the legal verbiage, Steadman said, "I've studied these matters, and I know the form is correct. What we never had before was the impetus to put it through. You've supplied that."

John Riggs added, "We were both of us up most of the night and again early this morning, pestering people and reading them your editorial. It's a damned shame this affair had to cost a boy his life; but, at least, it gave you a text and a chance to make them see something has to be done—and soon."

"You've certainly got a bunch of signatures," Tanner said. He was pleased to notice that of the Reverend James Lawless among the others.

"We didn't waste time on those Railroad Avenue speculators," Steadman said. "We wanted the businessmen, the people who actually count. And this time we wouldn't take no for an answer!"

Parley Newcome, looking past his employer's elbow, remarked

dryly, "Couple of names I don't seem to see—and I don't mean Morg DuShane's."

Doc Riggs readily agreed. "Beason and Nat Colby. . . . They already made it clear where they stand; we saw no point in bothering them. With all the others we've got, we can put this through in spite of them—and make them like it!"

"Maybe." Clark Tanner was a little dubious.

He had gone over the list a second time and now he pointed out, "I don't see Tom McDougall here either. Was he asked?"

Steadman, who was no friend of the gaunt livery owner, nodded sourly. "Sure, I asked him. He fussed around and finally turned me down cold. He's so thick with Virgil Beason, I knew there wasn't any real chance he'd sign."

"When was this?"

"Half hour ago, maybe."

Tanner said thoughtfully, "Then we can guess Beason and Colby will have the word by now, as to what's going on. It would be too big a risk, ignoring them completely. Beason's too clever; we might be sorry."

"So what do you suggest?"

"I'm not really sure. But I'm on my way over to their office now. Let me take this with me; I might have a chance to use it."

The hotel man hesitated. He was clearly reluctant. "All right—but don't let Beason get his hands on it, because he just might try to tear it up. John and I would just have to go and get the names again. And time is short."

"Agreed."

"Wait a minute," Parley Newcome broke in, as Tanner started to fold the petition and place it in his coat pocket. "Ain't you going to let me sign, first? Looks to me I'm as much a responsible citizen of Eden Grove as the next man—and if I am, by God, I want Beason to see my name there."

Tanner looked at him. "Sure. Fetch the pen; we'll both sign. . . ."

It came as no surprise, when he entered the town company office, to find Tom McDougall already there. The livery owner was hovering over the desk where Nat Colby and Virgil Beason were engrossed in a copy of the *Gazette*. All three looked up to watch, in a dead silence broken only by the uneven sound of his own limp, as Clark Tanner went through the partition gate and set down the bulky packet he had brought with him. "Here's a thousand more," he said without preliminary.

Nat Colby swore; a sweep of his heavy arm sent the bundle of newspapers off the desk, narrowly missing Tanner's lame hip. The cotton string Parley Newcome had tied around them snapped and a thousand sheets of newsprint spilled and drifted across the office floor. "One is a damn plenty!" Colby said, his thick features dark with anger. "You think anybody here is going to give you a dime for more?"

"According to the deal," Tanner answered coldly. "It was a firm order."

Virgil Beason, shrewd-eyed and with unrevealing expression, said, "He's right, Nat. I made a commitment."

"And I *told* you it was a mistake!" Colby snapped. "Putting good money into this paper of his, without knowing what he might be printing to undermine us. . . ."

Tanner said, without heat, "I've done nothing except to promote the best interests of Eden Grove."

Colby slapped a thick, work-toughened hand on the paper before him on the desk. "So some fool kid gets himself shot trying to hold up a legitimate place of business—and you make us out to be murderers!"

Clark Tanner considered him a moment, decided to let that go without an answer. Now Virgil Beason remarked with a jerk of his head at McDougall standing behind him, "Tom, here, says there's a petition going around on account of what you wrote. Do you know anything about it?"

In reply, Tanner removed it from his coat pocket, unfolded and laid it on the desk. But remembering Steadman's warning, he placed a hand on the paper and they had to read it where it lay, even Tom McDougall craning for a look across Beason's shoulder. Carefully studying the three faces, Tanner saw surprise and even a hint of consternation at the long tail of signatures filling most of the sheet. He saw Nat Colby's lips moving and thought the big man was counting under his breath.

Beason turned to look at the man standing behind him. "Tom," he said, too quietly, "you never mentioned they had so many signers."

The liveryman's bony features turned red. "I didn't know! I never really looked at the thing, Virg. Steadman come at me and shoved this newspaper under my nose and started talking petition. I shut him off—I just figured it would be the same as last time."

"It's *not* the same as last time," Clark Tanner said. "The town has changed."

Nat Colby said harshly, "And I suppose you take credit?"

"No. It was the killing of that boy. Overnight, because of it, the doc and Phil Steadman have put Eden Grove on record supporting organization, just as soon as the judge can be persuaded to move. They worked hard, but I don't think there's many they asked who weren't more than ready to sign."

"You'll notice one sonofabitch who did, Virg." The ring on Colby's hand flickered blue fire as a finger tapped a name— Tanner could see it was that of the store manager, Harolday. "Where does that fellow get the nerve to take our pay and then—?"

Clark Tanner interrupted, in a chill voice. "You might as well face facts, Colby. The ones who signed this paper don't want to see any more Hans Burkhalters shot down here, in cold blood. They want an orderly government—and they want it bad enough to put their names on the line, in spite of pressures or threats."

"Threats!" Virgil Beason repeated the word angrily. "Is there no end to that sort of talk, about Nat and me—as though either of us would want to hold the town back, when we've worked hard to bring it along *this* far! I know you've heard me say I didn't think these people were ready to levy taxes on themselves. Naturally I'm more than pleased to learn otherwise. Maybe this will prove it!" And he took up a pen, dipped it in the inkwell and added his name to the paper in a firm, clear hand.

"It would have seemed only fair," he commented as he wrote, "to give Nat and me a chance at the top of the list. But that can't be helped now." Finished writing, he thrust the pen at his cousin who looked at it as though he had never seen one before. He looked at Beason and then, with an expression of pure bewilderment, Nat Colby accepted the pen and made an almost unreadable scrawl. "Tom . . ." Beason jerked his head at McDougall; the liveryman, obviously at a loss, leaned over the desk and without a word followed suit.

"There! Are you satisfied now?" Beason looked at Tanner out

of his sly fox eyes, as he picked up the paper and waved it to dry the ink. "I know Judge Carver very well. When I go into Hutchinson on Monday, I'll be glad to deliver this to him personally." "No," Tanner said. "I don't think so." And he reached and took the petition from the other man's fingers. "Steadman and the doc won't be in favor of waiting till Monday, not when the railroad is due in little more than a week. Their idea is for a committee, in support of the petition; it's a long day's ride to Hutchinson, but by leaving this morning—as soon as possible, inside the hour—they just might reach the judge before he leaves his chambers and help put pressure on him. Once he sees the importance of it, they hope he'll be willing to co-operate."

"A committee!" Nat Colby grunted, with heavy sarcasm. "Steadman and Doc Riggs, I suppose. And naturally *you'll* be going."

Clark Tanner gave him a cool look. "I need to get the story for the paper, if nothing else."

The big man scowled. Virgil Beason had shown a flash of real anger as the petition was lifted out of his hand, but he quickly covered it. Now he seemed to reach a decision—he slapped both palms upon the desk as he said, "Very well. I told you, I know Carver; I'm sure I can get him to work with us. Nat and I, and Tom here—we'll all three join you on this committee. Getting the court's approval of our petition should be almost automatic."

So now it was "our" petition! Tanner met the bland regard of those shrewd eyes; he read bafflement in Nat Colby and Tom McDougall at what they must know was a complete about-face. Seeing himself outmaneuvered, Virgil Beason was bent on taking the initiative and in some way making it work to his advantage.

"That makes a six-man delegation," Clark Tanner pointed out. "Better if there's an odd number, in case we have to take a vote on something. I suggest we ask the preacher if he'd be willing to go along and make a seventh."

"Lawless . . ." Virgil Beason worked at the idea; Tanner could see the question in his eyes as he tested it for danger. But in the end, he could hardly do anything but agree. Having personally induced the minister to cast his fortunes with Eden Grove, and clinched the invitation with a free building lot, he must feel he had a claim to the man's support—at least, his neutrality. Tanner

doubted there was any other name he could offer that would have
had as good a chance being acceptable to both sides.

"All right," Beason said now, confirming this guess. "We'll ask
him. In any event, we should leave as soon as possible for end of
track; with luck we'll find a supply train returning empty, so we
can deadhead in to Hutchinson and save hours of travel time.
And afterward"—he was suddenly smiling; the hint of a gold
tooth glimmered as he rubbed dry palms together—"afterward, if
our mission goes as I expect it to, I want you to tell the others
that the entire committee is to be my guests for dinner, to celebrate—at the best restaurant in town."

Clark Tanner stared at him, but he seemed entirely serious.
Tanner nodded slowly. "Fine," he said. "I'll pass the word." The
expressions on Beason's friends amused him; if anything they were
more startled than he was by the man's complete change of atti-
tude. Starting for the door, booting through the drift of newspapers Nat Colby had scattered, he could sense the questions
building to be unleashed on Virgil Beason, the moment they were
alone. . . .

And now it was twelve eventful hours later, and Beason's idea
of the best eating place in Hutchinson had turned out to be the
hotel's private dining room. Certainly it beat anything Eden
Grove could boast, with its turkey-red carpet and wallpaper and
the oil lamps with their tastefully painted shades. A table had
been set beforehand, snowy linen and real silver and long-
stemmed water glasses; everything seemed prepared for a truly special evening.

When Clark Tanner walked in, just before eight-thirty, he
found Phil Steadman and John Riggs ahead of him but, as yet, no
member of Beason's group. After ceremonial handshakes, Steadman produced a box of cigars; Tanner accepted a couple with
thanks, and put them in his pocket for after dinner.

Riggs seemed in a poor mood. "All right," he said shortly, in
reply to a comment from Steadman. "I admit it—we finally got
what we've been campaigning for. Thanks to Tanner, here, Beason even got pushed into a corner where he had to stop fighting
us and help put it through. But—"

"But what?" Phil Steadman demanded. "Why are you grous-

ing, now? You'll only spoil your appetite for what promises to be a
damn sight better meal than you'll ever get at *my* place—and
Beason's picking up the tab for it!"

"That's just what bothers me," Riggs said, through a furious
cloud of cigar smoke. "He gave in too easy! There's something up
his sleeve—and I'm just wondering when we're going to find out
what it is."

"Nobody's taking anything for granted," his friend assured him.
"Don't worry. We'll have our guard up. But you've got to admit
there's reason to celebrate, all the same."

Clark Tanner asked, "Has anyone seen Lawless?"

"Not since we left the judge's chambers," Steadman said. "He
was with Beason then, wasn't he?"

There was a sound of voices out in the hallway, just then, and
Nat Colby and Tom McDougall entered.

To Tanner, Colby's peasant features looked more flushed than
usual; he had likely been drinking, but it hadn't made him any
pleasanter. His manner was roughly belligerent and the lantern-
jawed livery stable owner was in no friendlier mood. But before
anyone could speak, on either side, Virgil Beason's voice boomed
through the hall and he came in with James Lawless in tow. He
looked around, nodded in hearty approval. "We're all here, I see.
What do you say we get right to it? I think I could eat a steer!"
Playing the host he hustled them all to the table, himself taking
the place at the head of it. A waiter appeared with an expensive-
looking bottle; Beason told his guests, "I thought champagne was
called for. Reverend, you won't refuse to join us, I hope."

"For a special occasion," Jim Lawless said, smiling a little, "I
suppose I can make an exception this once. Just don't anyone tell
my sister."

Beason poured and called for a toast. "Gentlemen, I give you
Eden Grove—as of this date of July 19, 1872, the newest city of
the third class in the state of Kansas!" And for all their suspicions
as to his ultimate purposes, that was one salute in which every
man at the table was glad enough to join.

The meal was excellent—steak under onions, all the trimmings.
Beason kept the talk alive and the wine glasses filled, his gold
tooth gleaming as he maintained a lively banter; but, to Tanner's
watchful observation, the eyes in his narrow fox face remained

shrewdly on watch, unaltered by the show of high good feelings. And though Tanner enjoyed the meal and the champagne, he never came close to letting down his own guard.

Something was coming—he felt sure of it; he caught John Riggs's eye from time to time, across the loaded table, and read the same thought there.

Then Virgil Beason was rapping on his wine glass with a table knife, calling for attention. "Another toast," he announced. "Are we all ready?" The question was superfluous. He had been keeping the glasses full for everyone, except Lawless who had never emptied his. Lifting his own, Beason said, "I give you a man of vision, a man without whom there would be no Eden Grove today . . . Nat Colby!"

This time there was real meaning in the look that passed between Tanner and the doctor. Riggs lifted one shoulder in a shrug and picked up his glass; reluctantly, Tanner did the same. Colby, seated at Beason's right, accepted the tribute with a smirk and tried to appear modest.

"I have a suggestion to offer," Beason said then, and Tanner suddenly knew they had reached the moment for which the food and the wine had only been a preparation. "Now that the court has appointed this delegation to act as Eden Grove's first governing body, I think it would be fitting to declare a council meeting in session—right here—and elect a mayor for our town. And it seems obvious there's nobody more deserving the honor than the one who brought Eden Grove into being."

Promptly, as though on cue, Tom McDougall echoed him: "Nat Colby. . . . I'll second that nomination. I move we make it unanimous."

Taken by surprise, their minds perhaps a little numbed by food and wine, no one else spoke immediately. Beason seemed to take that for approval and proceeded to ram the thing through. "Why not? A good idea, Tom," he said expansively. "If there are no objections—"

"Just a moment."

The interruption caught him in midsentence. He stiffened and his head turned sharply, as a cold stare sought out Clark Tanner. The latter had placed both palms on the tablecloth; he continued, evenly, "No point rushing things. If this is a meeting and we're making nominations, I have one to offer. I'd merely like to point out—we wouldn't even be sitting here, with any need for choosing a mayor, if one man in particular hadn't kept up the battle to have Eden Grove legally organized. For that reason I nominate Phil Steadman."

"Seconded," John Riggs said calmly.

It had been Virgil Beason's turn to be caught off guard. The only one on his feet, he stood eyeing Tanner as though, by the sheer weight of his displeasure, he could make the latter retract what he had said. Tanner returned the look, and after a moment Beason drew a breath and, in a voice that he wasn't quite able to hold steady, told the table, "Very well. We would seem to be split evenly, down the middle. If there are no further nominations, it looks as though we'll have to call for a vote to break the tie. . . ."

Almost in unison, heads turned and the attention of the table focused on James Lawless.

You could almost see understanding of the situation dawn on him. He straightened a little in his chair; his glance ran from face to face, meeting their looks and plainly figuring for himself the way the tally would have to run—three for either candidate, with his deciding vote the only one in doubt. Tanner saw him frown, and felt a sudden gnawing uncertainty.

Suddenly he wondered just how much he really knew about this man—or just what he and Virgil Beason might have been up to, in the time since they left Judge Carver's chambers together. If Lawless' sympathies, or a sense of obligation, made him vote with Beason's party, there could be far-reaching consequences for all of them and for Eden Grove itself.

Clark Tanner felt his breath go tight in his throat.

"Is it really up to me?" James Lawless exclaimed then. He shook his head. "I'll admit it's not a role I like to play, but I won't try to get out of it. All I can do is vote for the one I consider the most experienced, and the best qualified to hold the office. I hope you all understand I don't mean any reflection on anyone." He hesitated, while they all waited. And he finished: "So I'll have to say, my vote goes to Mr. Steadman. . . ."

For a moment Tanner was aware of the sound of his own shallow breathing, of a murmur of voices in other reaches of the building, even the clatter of pans in the kitchen, removed by several intervening partitions from this room. John Riggs was the first one to break the stillness; he suddenly reached a hand across the table to his friend, telling Steadman, "Congratulations, Mayor!"

Nat Colby showed the effects of shock: First his ruddy features turned chalk-white, and then angry color flooded them. His mouth opened; he seemed set for some angry outburst, when Virgil Beason's hand dropped on his meaty shoulder with a pressure that silenced him. Beason looked a little pale, himself, and the lines that bracketed his mouth were pulled deep; but he had his voice under control as he said, "Well . . . that seems to be settled." He didn't suggest a toast now, Tanner noticed; he was suddenly brusque, as though he wanted to bring this to an end as quickly as possible. "Nothing much more to be done tonight, I suppose."

"I'll agree with that," Phil Steadman said, also coming to his feet. He had the good sense not to push his victory; all business, he said simply, "Why don't the bunch of us get together in my office at the hotel on Monday morning and set things rolling? I'd say the first priority is a special assessment on the town's businesses, to meet starting salaries and expenses."

Nat Colby found his voice. There was sneering hostility in it as he asked the man who had beaten him, "Just how big a salary you figuring for yourself?"

Phil Steadman returned the challenging look coolly enough; he could probably judge the big man's disappointment at missing out by a single vote, and he wasn't inclined to rub it in. "I wouldn't accept a penny," he answered. "I consider the post an honor and payment enough. What's more, I'm assuming that no man in this group expects anything for his services, not at least until some time when the citizens of Eden Grove have had a say in electing him."

"Absolutely right," the doctor agreed. "It's bad enough we were appointed over their heads and that they're stuck with us."

Steadman continued: "When I speak of salaries, I mean that we need a police force—and we need it as soon as possible. We have to be especially careful, filling the town marshal's post; we can't risk a fiasco like the one at Abilene last year, when Wild Bill Hickok used his badge to go after his personal enemies."

"I think I know just the man," Virgil Beason put in quickly. Was he trying to salvage some of his lost control? Tanner wondered.

If Steadman saw what the man was up to, he gave him no satisfaction. On the other hand, he wouldn't go so far as to say outright that he wasn't apt to be interested in anyone Virgil Beason might suggest; instead he told them, "I've got a name or two in mind, myself. I'll have a list drawn up by Monday, and if we can agree on a salary, I'll start writing letters. Meanwhile, I can't think of anything else needs bringing up tonight, so we might as well adjourn. It's been a long day."

And, in fact, with the meal finished and this business concluded, no one seemed inclined to drag matters out any longer. Beason, plainly vexed over the way his plans had backfired, left without so much as giving anyone a chance to thank him for the dinner; John Riggs told Tanner, in a dry voice, "He's going to be wondering, for a long time, just what happened. He thought he had it all set up for Colby."

Tanner, getting slowly to his feet because that left hip was paining him a bit more than usual, was watching a little scene being enacted by Nat Colby and the minister. Lawless had managed to intercept the big man at the door, and there was a terse exchange —the preacher speaking earnestly, Colby listening with a scowl on his ruddy face, and then shrugging and tossing out some angry word before he turned and ducked into the hall. Lawless was shaking his head over the matter when Tanner joined him.

"I suppose the man will never forgive me, voting the way I did," he said regretfully. "But I couldn't do anything else. Colby simply isn't smart enough for the mayor's job."

Tanner said, "If his nose is out of joint, it can't be helped—you did what you had to. And with the railroad almost due, there are more important things to concern us than Nat Colby's hurt feelings. I wouldn't worry about it. . . ."

# CHAPTER XIV

Notable occasions, Clark Tanner was thinking, often failed to provide their proper settings. Nobody could say that this twenty-ninth of July was an improvement on the days that had come before, or were apt to follow. Early, a high film of clouds turned the sun into a brassy smear but did little to break its force; by nine o'clock the town already lay panting under the assault, but the men of Eden Grove, being inured to Kansas weather, paid it little mind. As ten-thirty neared, the sweltering expanse of Railroad Avenue was already beginning to stir with life.

A few farm wagons had been coming off the prairie, as a thin scattering of homesteaders brought their families in for the occasion. Dust cut by iron-rimmed wheels lifted and hung in the town's motionless air; there was no wind at all, and the bunting that had been strung on the building fronts facing Railroad Avenue, and on the bare plank speakers' stand erected near the depot, hung limp. But now, with a half hour to go before the scheduled ceremony, a squawl of brass and the thumping of a drum began to sound; and that was the signal. Eden Grove began to gather, drawn to the sound as by a magnet.

The town had no band of its own, so one had been hired and brought out from Hutchinson. Seated on the speakers' platform, it didn't look like much of a band—two trumpets, a tuba, a piccolo, a bass drum; but when the first notes began to echo thinly in the midmorning stillness they lifted the pulse of everyone who heard them, as the sound of band music—good or bad—never fails to do. Doors slammed, boots pounded wooden sidewalks. Within minutes, a bigger crowd than Clark Tanner would have thought Eden Grove could muster started converging on the open space before the speakers' stand.

Dust settled on faces and clothing and sifted in under collars.

Hot sunlight glittered on the brass of instruments blown by red-faced and sweating musicians. It made eye-punishing liquid streaks of the new iron rails that skewered the length of Railroad Avenue, to halt, abruptly, a quarter mile west of the village, where the Santa Fe had installed a switch and a rather clumsy-looking turntable for reversing the big diamond-stacked engines. Kids off the homesteader wagons ran wild through the crowd; dogs barked; a horse at a hitching rail pitched up a sudden ruckus when some-one unloaded a firecracker under it, saved over from the Fourth.

There were only a few women—the girls from Cotton's place, and farmers' wives in faded homespun and wing bonnets. As Tanner stood with Parley Newcome under the wooden awning of Whitfield's drugstore, he looked for the Burkhalters but was not much surprised when he failed to see them. Emil Burkhalter was not likely, on a Monday, to drop his work and bring his family to town just for the frivolous purpose of watching the first arrival of the Santa Fe cars.

Sam Harolday and his family appeared, Harolday bearing him-self with his usual imposing manner, Lucy looking cool in spite of the day. She had an inadequate trinket of a parasol lifted in one hand while the other kept her full, light blue skirt clear of the dust; the little girl, a miniature of the mother, walked gravely and sedately between her parents. Tanner watched them mingle with the mill of people in the sunlit street.

He settled the hang of his coat, then checked the wad of news-print in one pocket for taking notes, shifted slightly the revolver tucked behind his waistband. He was never without that gun, these days, when he ventured on the streets of this town—not while Morgan DuShane was a part of it; though if DuShane had ideas of seeking retaliation for the comments in the *Gazette* about the killing of young Burkhalter, he was taking his time about it. Tanner had never once run into him, face to face, since the story was printed. He had about decided the man was merely biding his time, letting him stew. . . .

He told Newcome, "Well, I guess I'd better go out there and circulate, get the color of this for my story."

Parley Newcome positioned himself more comfortably, easing one shoulder against a support of the shading roof. "You go right

ahead," he said complacently. "I can get all the color I need from
here. A sun like that can render the lard right out of you!"

Leaving him, Tanner moved out into the street and threaded a
path through the bustling crowd toward the speakers' stand. He
nodded or spoke to people he knew, and once got a shout and a
wave of one thick raised arm from Peter Duffy. The fat man was
sweating and grinning with excitement; Tanner knew that after
today he was expecting to see his business doubled, thanks to hungry passengers who would be tumbling off the cars and looking for
a place to eat. Duffy was talking, these days, of building an addition to his restaurant, adding more tables, bringing in a full-time
cook to free himself from his bondage at stove and lunch counter.

Tanner stopped and they talked for a moment. Duffy had a
bottle and, like others in the crowd, was doing some celebrating
ahead of time; he offered Tanner a drink but the latter declined,
with a smile. "It's all well and good for you," he pointed out.
"But I'm just a newspaperman, on the job."

"That's a fact," Peter Duffy agreed. "They'd have us believe
we're makin' history, so you best be sure you get it right!"

As he approached the speakers' stand, the thump of the bass
drum grew more persistent until Tanner could feel it throbbing in
his bones. He came upon Kit Lawless and her brother listening to
the music. When she turned and saw him, her whole face lit up
with unfeigned pleasure, in a way that warmed him through. Her
hand squeezed his as she said, putting her mouth close to his ear
to make herself heard above the instruments, "Aren't they *awful!*"

"Pretty terrible," Tanner agreed, wincing at a sour blast from
the second trumpet. "They were the best Hutchinson could
scrape together for us. But maybe, one of these days, Eden Grove
will be able to have a brass band of its own that's just as bad."

The number ended, to applause and shouts of approval from
those who sounded as though they'd been celebrating with special
vigor. The stillness after the steady thump of the drum was not allowed to last for long; the band struck up again. Tanner would
rather have stayed where he was, with the girl's hand in his, but
he had his job to do; he excused himself and left her there with
her brother.

Lawless called after him, followed a step or two to ask, in some
concern, "Have you seen that man DuShane?"

Tanner shook his head.

"He's in the crowd somewhere, with Beason. It appeared to me he'd been drinking, and with a man like that you can never predict what it might put into his head to do. After what you said in the paper . . ."

Tanner pointed out, "It's been over a week and he's done nothing. But, thanks for the warning. I'll be careful."

"I hope so." Tanner didn't know if the other was aware he carried a gun under his coat. He thanked Lawless again and left him, angling now toward the small, and still unpainted, depot.

He kept an eye open for DuShane but failed to discover him. He estimated there must be over two hundred people collected in this dusty, open street. A lot of whiskey bottles were being emptied. In spite of the heat and the waiting, the mood was generally a good one, but anything could turn it. At one place in the crowd a sudden eddy of disturbance marked where a couple of men had fallen into an argument. Whatever the issue, blows were struck, yells went up; but friends separated the brawlers before real harm was done.

These men had been marking time, through long and frustrating weeks of waiting for a day that had finally arrived. Now they meant to celebrate, and they were getting noisier by the minute.

Stepping over shining rails and newly laid ballast, Tanner gained the depot and found Phil Steadman pacing the cinders and sweltering in his best clothes. The mayor of Eden Grove looked sadly ill at ease. "I'm not so sure right now I should thank you for getting me into this," he told Tanner. "I've never made a speech in my life. Should have made you write this one for me!" He had some words scribbled on sheets of paper and was mumbling them over, rehearsing for the ordeal ahead.

Tanner, amused, said, "You don't really think anyone's going to be listening? They can read it all in the *Gazette*, later—and if it needs rewriting I'll polish it up for you."

"Mostly pompous nonsense anyway," Steadman muttered. "And, God! Is it hot!" He dug out a handkerchief to swab at his sweating face and at his neck that looked pinched and uncomfortable in a stiff collar and four-in-hand. Tanner thought that Sam Harolday, with his façade of stiff and phony dignity, would have looked better; Phil Steadman had an air of competence and his own kind of dignity, but hardly suited to an occasion like this.

Tanner said encouragingly, "You shouldn't have to wait much longer. With a lot of officials on board, they can hardly afford to let that train be too far off schedule—not on its very first run. . . ."

As though on cue, the band wound up another number just then and into its wake the long, faint ghost of a steam whistle sounded, somewhere eastward. All at once men, perched on vantage points along the roofs of buildings, were pointing and shouting. Tanner stepped out onto the right-of-way—now, squinting against the liquid streaks of the tracks running away from where he stood, he made out a white drift of smoke pluming and dissolving to the rhythmic pant of a still invisible engine.

Eden Grove had become used to the sight and sound of work trains, but this could only mean one thing. The crowd pressed forward, with new excitement, and Phil Steadman quickly had his hands full.

He was everywhere at once, giving orders, trying to hold back the mob while he got the musicians down off the speakers' stand and lined up in some kind of formation. A welcoming committee took their places, chiefly the court-appointed members of the city council; catching sight of Virgil Beason and Nat Colby, the latter scowling as though at some grievance of his own, Tanner was reminded again of Morgan DuShane. He looked about for Du-Shane but failed to spot him in the crowd.

The train was close now, the engineer leaning on his whistle and clanging his bell. Suddenly, rounding a curve, the big diamond stack came roaring into view, drive wheels pounding the earth but already slowing as it swept out upon the creek trestle.

There was not a lot to the first train at Eden Grove—besides engine, tender, and caboose, nothing but a single coach and baggage car. Still, it would serve its symbolic purpose. With screech of brake shoes and crash of couplings it groaned and settled to a halt; there it stood, reeking of smoke and hot metal and panting steam, while the heated air shook and danced above the boiler. And now, the frantic cheering of the crowd and the slamming of the drum and thin squawk of the trumpets could, at last, be heard.

A trio of representatives from the Santa Fe Railroad climbed down the steps of the coach, to be greeted.

They could hardly have expected anyone of very great importance, but Eden Grove had at least rated the division superintendent and two minor officials from Kansas City. Tanner, with a newspaperman's training, recorded and stored away names and titles in the few moments while introductions were made and handshakes exchanged; then, without more ado, Phil Steadman was leading his guests to the steps of the speakers' stand. Clark Tanner hung back, more interested in observing what went on than playing a part in it.

Other passengers, perhaps a dozen, had followed the railroad officials off the coach. He looked them over, making his guesses as to their personal reasons for wanting to be aboard this particular train. More speculators for the most part, he judged; though he wondered if one or two might not be independent cattle buyers, or men from commission houses, here to look into the possibilities of Eden Grove developing into a center for the Texas trade. Others had the obvious earmarks of sales drummers, identifiable not only by their sample cases but by a certain aggressiveness in their clothing and their manner.

Then he saw the woman.

She was noticeable, for seeming to be alone; there had been others in the group, but those had all been in the company of males—they might even have been their wives, in some cases, though some just as clearly were not. But if this one traveled without escort, neither did she have the look of Lew Cotton's girls. She was conservatively dressed, slightly rumpled from the coach and from the July heat but still with something collected and reserved about her. She carried a reticule and there was a small traveling bag at her feet; she stood, a few yards away from him, surveying the noisy scene in front of her.

Whatever her reason for coming to Eden Grove, she seemed unsure of the next step. She turned her head and her eyes met Tanner's and held on him for a moment—dark eyes, in a pale face made paler by contrast to the shining brown wings of hair visible beneath the edge of her bonnet. She had a good figure; he would judge her somewhere toward the middle of her thirties. He thought she might be about to speak to him and lifted a hand to touch his hatbrim. But when he did that, she turned abruptly away again and leaned for her traveling bag. As he watched she started walking from the cars and the railroad tracks, at an angle though the crowd as she made for the buildings on the north side of the street.

Up on the platform, the visiting officials had been introduced and now one of them had launched into a speech. After two sentences Clark Tanner stopped listening because that had been enough to tell him how his story in the *Gazette* would certainly read:

> . . . At Monday's ceremony marking arrival of the Atchison, Topeka & Santa Fe at this place, Howard Williamson, a vice-president for the railroad, told an appreciative audience that the city of Eden Grove faced a future of great promise, as the undoubted center for the Texas cattle business and the hub of an agricultural area.
>
> We were given assurances that his company offers every support to the prospects and anticipations of this city for prosperity and growth in the years ahead.
>
> Can anyone doubt, with its favorable location and many natural advantages, that Eden Grove is indeed destined to become the metropolis of the Arkansas River Valley, and an exemplar for other communities? . . .

But Tanner's mind was really no more than half on his work. He found himself frowning at the place where that unknown woman had disappeared into the jostling crowd. Something about her intrigued him; perhaps it was a newsman's sixth sense for the possibility of a story . . . or perhaps merely a feeling that an attractive woman, alone, might discover a place like this town—on this day in particular—more than she had bargained for. . . .

For whatever reason, he suddenly put his back to the activities around the speakers' platform and started in the direction the woman had taken. It was as though she had been swallowed up; but then he elbowed his way past someone who cursed him, boozily, and suddenly he saw her. A big fellow in a bowler hat and unbuttoned waistcoat and sweat-blackened shirt blocked her path.

He loomed over her, a simpering grin on his sweating face, and Tanner saw him place a hand on the woman's arm.

Alarmed, Tanner moved forward in such haste that a stitch of agony in the injured hip halted him and nearly doubled him over. He never knew with certainty what happened—whether she said something, or her disdainful look was enough to bring the man to heel. But the big fellow had stepped aside, his grin erased, and the woman was sweeping past him without so much as another look. Whoever she was, she knew how to handle herself.

Clark Tanner, still curious, reached a farm wagon someone had left in front of the big hotel. He paused there, to rest a hand on the edge of the wagonbox while he eased his weight off the aching hip, and watched to see what the woman would do.

She appeared to have decided to ask someone for information. Tom McDougall lounged in the door of his livery barn where, with hands in hip pockets, gaunt jaws working on a chew of tobacco, he had been aloofly watching the events in the street; though a member of the city council, McDougall had seemed to take less and less interest in Eden Grove's affairs since he became convinced Phil Steadman and his friends were taking over control of them. Now, as the woman halted before him, he brushed a palm across his short fringe of beard while he listened to whatever she was asking and gave her a slow stare, from head to foot. He appeared to ask a question of his own, and at her answer shrugged and shook his head.

Whatever it was she wanted to know, she had failed to learn it here. After a few more words Tanner watched her look about uncertainly and then turn in the direction of the hotel. As she mounted the lobby steps, on an impulse he ducked around the tailgate of the wagon and went after her.

There was no clerk on duty. Alone there, the woman had placed her reticule on the desk and set her bag at her feet. He saw the wary look she gave him and quickly sought to put her at her ease; keeping his distance, he took off his hat and introduced himself. "I don't want to seem forward, ma'am," he added. "But I couldn't help seeing you get off the train, just now, with no one to meet you. I'm afraid that today, especially, this can be a rough town for a woman all by herself."

She studied him a moment with eyes as dark as her hair. She

was older then he'd thought, and her face held certain marks of hardship or anxiety; but she was still, he thought, decidedly attractive. He said, "Perhaps you're looking for someone. . . ."

She seemed to make a decision. "Yes," she answered. "I am, as a matter of fact. And you're a newspaperman? Then you ought to know as much about this town as anyone."

"That might be a matter of opinion. But you can try me."

"Converse—William Converse. Does the name mean anything to you?"

He had to shake his head. "I'm afraid not. Can you tell me anything more?"

She was opening her reticule. "I have his picture, taken a little over a year ago. I'm Rose Converse; he's my husband."

Suddenly Tanner was wishing he hadn't interfered. He accepted the picture, with some reluctance; it showed him the woman and a man, posed stiffly against a studio background of a painted landscape and artfully broken Grecian pillar—she smiling and attractive, in happier circumstances than today; the man, handsome enough. Tanner judged him to be forty or a year or two older, with receding sandy hair and a hawkish cast to his face. The eyes, in the photograph, seemed strangely pale and piercing. Both people were well dressed. The cardboard frame was stamped with the name of a Dallas photographer's studio.

He studied the picture during a long moment. Actually he was stalling, reluctant to deal with a deserted wife who had chased an errant husband all the way from Texas. He wondered what he would do if she began to cry, although, to give her credit, she didn't seen at all the crying type. Finally, with a shake of the head he told her, "I'm sorry, Mrs. Converse. I don't remember ever seeing him—and I see quite a lot of faces, from one day to another. What's his line of work?"

She looked him squarely in the eye, without flinching. "Not to put too fine a face on it, Mr. Tanner, he is a gambler. A professional—and a good one."

"Oh." Tanner tried to keep the stiffness out of his manner as he handed back the picture. "Well, I'm very much afraid there's little I can do except wish you luck."

Coldly, not looking at him as she replaced the bit of cardboard in her reticule, she said, "I can tell what you're thinking, Mr.

Tanner—I'm used to it. But you happen to be wrong. I am not a deserted woman. My husband may be restless; I knew it when I married him, and I knew he would never change. But we have been married for ten years, and wherever he was he has always seen to it I was well taken care of. In his own way—in the only way he knows—Will Converse is a good provider and a good husband!"

Tanner felt his jaws grow warm. "Ma'am, I never said . . ."

"No, it was in what you *didn't* say." She met his look then, and in spite of the strength he sensed in her it seemed for once that she might actually be close to tears. "I was too quick to take offense. I'm sorry. I won't trouble you further."

She turned and he watched her as she moved away from him. A sagging horsehair sofa stood by the lobby's plate glass window; she rested a hand on its back while she looked out into the sunblasted street and at the crowd clustered about the speakers' stand where the day's ceremony continued. She looked desperately alone, and even frightened; and impulsively Tanner went limping after her.

"I'm the one that ought to apologize," he said. "I shouldn't have jumped to conclusions. But as for your husband, if he's really a professional this hardly seems the place he'd have come. So far there's more talk than money, here; he wouldn't see any real action until the trail herds begin stopping and paying off their crews, and the cattle buyers and commission house men come to do business. You'd be better advised to do your looking at Ellsworth, or Abilene, or Wichita—places where the markets are already in operation."

Her attention still on the view beyond the window, she shook her head and answered dully, "I've been to those places. You just haven't heard the whole story."

"Then maybe I should. Would you want to tell it to me?" As she hesitated, he indicated the sofa. "We can talk better sitting down. . . ."

He was glad when she decided to agree; it was easy to misjudge how much he could demand of that injured leg. Seated beside the woman, his hat on his knee, he prompted her: "When was the last you heard from your husband, Mrs. Converse?"

"It was last summer—almost a year ago," she said, and the life seemed to have gone out of her voice; one could go only so long on nerve and hope. "He sent me money from St. Louis, and told me he was going on to Abilene, where he had friends among the Texas drovers; they would be closing deals for their herds by then, and there should be plenty of cash around. He expected to be home before Christmas. He never came—and I never heard another word from him."

"Anyone you could check with?" Tanner suggested. "His friends . . ."

"Naturally, I wrote everyone I could think of. Several told me that he *was* at Abilene; they'd seen him playing there and his luck seemed to be running. But that was all I did learn.

"I was ill during the winter; it was months before I became strong enough to travel. As soon as I was able, I came north to look for myself. . . ."

Worry added to the effects of illness, Tanner thought, explained the changes in her face since the photograph was taken—the dark stains beneath her eyes, the lines about her mouth. "It's a long journey," he said slowly, "for a woman traveling alone." By stage to New Orleans, he supposed, and then up by riverboat and across Kansas by rail. "And you found out nothing?"

"I know he went from Abilene west to Ellsworth, and that he was there until sometime in October. He has a friend who owns a saloon in Ellsworth. I talked to this man, and he told me my husband bought a horse and headed directly for Texas. Apparently he had quite a lot of money on him."

Tanner's eyes narrowed. Almost without thinking of its effect on the woman he exclaimed, "Anybody who knew that could have trailed him south."

But she emphatically shook her head. "His friend said he was too careful—that it isn't likely anyone knew. Still, my husband was concerned about what he might run into, if he should take the usual route through Newton and Wichita. He said he might decide to bypass them by keeping to the open prairie, west of such places; there'd be less chance of meeting anyone—at least, anyone who would know him and guess what he was carrying.

"I checked at Newton and Wichita, Mr. Tanner. There's no sign at all that he went that way. But I got word about this town of Eden Grove, that I'd never even heard of. I thought it could be worth having a look at it . . . You might almost say, a last resort."

Clark Tanner rubbed a hand across his jaw as he considered what she had told him. "If Converse rode south and west from Ellsworth," he said slowly, "he'd likely hit the old trader's trail—in which case he could have forded the Arkansas at just about this point, all right. But last October, he wouldn't have seen a town. Eden Grove didn't exist then; the plat wasn't even filed until sometime in January.

"So," he concluded reluctantly, as he got to his feet and stood looking down at the woman, "I don't know what else I can tell you. There's a lot of miles between here and Texas, through some wild and tough country. I'm afraid it's all too likely the answer to your husband's disappearance lies somewhere in that direction."

She stared at him like one stricken. And then her mouth lost its shape and she dropped her eyes from his, bowing her head to look at the hands twisted together in her lap. "I'm sorry," Clark Tanner said lamely, when she made no effort to answer him.

A thin spattering of applause ran through the crowd out there in the street, under the smash of the high sun. Tanner lifted his hands and dropped them at his sides. He shook his head and turned and left her.

# CHAPTER XV

It took no more than a few drinks to hone the edge of natural cruelty in Virgil Beason, and sharpen his sarcasm. When he came upon Nat Colby in the crowd below the speakers' platform and saw the sour look on his cousin, his own narrow face took on a twisted grin. "So what's eating you? I thought this was the day you'd been waiting for."

Colby had been holding it in too long. "Goddamn it!" he exploded, with hoarse indignation. "It's *my* town! I should be the one up there, making the speeches!"

Beason's grin turned to a sneer, the gold tooth gleaming. "What kind of a speech would *you* make? All you'd do is make a fool of yourself."

The other glared at him blackly and at Morgan DuShane who observed his anger with cool mockery. There were times, under the prodding of his cousin's superior manner and quicker intelligence, when Colby would gladly have taken Virgil Beason in his big hands and twisted him in two; but somehow he knew it would be a mistake. Colby had always been dimly afraid of his cousin. He sensed that Beason, for all the difference in their sizes, was dangerous; and the past weeks since he became so thick with this man DuShane, who carried a gun under his coat and a reputation for using it, had made it clearer than ever.

So with an angry shrug Colby turned away and left the pair of them. He didn't intend waiting to hear the applause for Phil Steadman, who was on the second page of his written speech. Nat Colby suddenly knew what he wanted—a drink; even if Cotton's place was closed, there was a bottle in a drawer on his desk at the land company office, and that would serve.

But Cotton's proved to be open, and he set his course for there. The long room was gratefully cool after the blast of the street; as his eyes adjusted to the dim light he saw that it was empty except for a bored bartender, a single drinking customer who stood with elbow on counter and boot on brass rail, and someone else who sat at a back table over a spread of solitaire. The one at the bar turned his head as Colby approached, and he recognized Tom McDougall. "Well!" the liveryman said dryly, his deep voice chasing echoes through the room. "Did you finally get enough oratory to last you?"

Colby grimaced as he signaled the bartender to fill a glass. "Big talk!" he said grumpily. "If that crowd out there really wanted to know what it took to build this town, why didn't they come to the man who had the vision? And who put the work and the sweat into making a city grow where there wasn't nothing before. . . ."

"Hardest work you've done, sitting in that office," a voice said gruffly, "was learning to spell your name!"

Truculent and ready for argument, Nat Colby spun away from the bar. He could see now that the man at the table was Parley Newcome, who was methodically laying out some complex pattern requiring two packs of cards, and giving his whole attention to it. He had a glass in front of him, filled to the brim with amber whiskey—one might almost believe he had set himself a challenge to see how long he could let it sit untouched. From the first encounter, Colby had dismissed this man contemptuously as little better than a common drunk; but he had an uncomfortable feeling that Newcome was just as contemptuous of *him*. Now, having made his comment, he acted as though he didn't even know Nat Colby was in the room.

Angry and frustrated, Colby only belatedly grew aware of what Tom McDougall was saying to him. "She was a real looker, too," the liveryman observed. "Sort of wished I could help, even if it was a husband she was asking for. But wasn't really anything I could tell her."

"What the hell you talking about, Tom?" Colby interrupted, irritably.

"This woman that got off the train. Ain't you been listening? I been telling you how she said she came all the way from Texas—alone, hunting the fellow she's married to that never made it home last year."

Nat Colby frowned, finding it difficult as usual to gear his slow thinking into a new line of discussion. "It's her husband she's looking for? And she expected to find him here?"

"Or word of him, maybe. I gather it was sort of a last chance try. But the description didn't sound like anybody I'd ever seen, and it was a name I never heard of. Cavanaugh . . . or—no: Converse. Yes, that was it. . . ."

A cold chill began to work in Nat Colby, grew to an insidious tightening of his gut. Suddenly his throat was dry; he fumbled for the glass on the bar in front of him and drained it off, all but choking on the stuff. *Converse.* . . . It was the name on the letters he'd taken from a dead man's saddlebags, letters that began, "Dearest Will . . ."

"This woman—" he managed to get out, in a voice that didn't sound much like his own. "Where did she go, after she finished with you?"

"The hotel. I saw that fellow Tanner go in behind her—maybe they talked and maybe they didn't, but he came out again right afterward. Later, as I was turning in here I saw her go past me, down the street. Struck me she could have been headed for your office—I'd told her that was one other place she might ask. . . ."

Colby put down his empty glass, mumbled something, and walked out of there leaving McDougall standing.

He caught sight of the woman while he was still almost a block away—with the ceremony at the speakers' stand continuing, the sidewalk here was nearly deserted. From the way she stood indecisively before the town company office, he thought she must have tried the door and, finding it locked, was pondering a next step. As he hastily closed the distance, Nat Colby's feelings swelled to an odd mix of anger and fear and a kind of disbelieving resentment at the turn things were taking. After all these months . . .

She turned as he halted beside her. "Ma'am?" he said gruffly. "I'm one of the partners in this office, if you're looking to do business. Let me open up, and we can step inside and discuss it."

"Thank you," she began. "It isn't business, exactly. But someone did suggest—"

He didn't give her time to finish; somehow he felt that he wanted her off the street, away from curious eyes, while they had this out. One panicky instant he wished for his cousin—Virg

would know better how to handle this situation—but as he fumbled at the padlock with his key, he told himself he didn't need
Virgil Beason.

What the hell! Was he afraid of a female half his size? All he
needed to do was watch his tongue—best yet, simply claim ignorance of any question she might ask.

The office, having been shut since the night before, was stifling.
Nevertheless, when he had ushered Will Converse's wife in, he
carefully closed the door again despite the stuffy heat. "Now then,
ma'am. . . ." Turning to her, with her eyes upon him, he was
suddenly struck by this woman's definite good looks. Taken aback,
he could not deny an impulse to make sure she understood his
own importance. "Nat Colby's the name," he told her, thrusting
out a hand. "I started this town—built it from nothin'. So—"

But she was no longer looking at his face. As they stood there in
the shadowy office, her stare had been drawn to the hand and to
the pale blue gleam of the ring he wore on it, shining faintly even
in this half light.

The formal ceremony was over, the last speech made to desul-
tory applause. The band was pumping away again and a few
firecrackers were going off, and the diamond stack let loose answering blasts from its whistle; but no one wanted to linger any
longer than they had to in the hot sunblast, and already the crowd
was breaking and scattering for shade—chiefly, the nearest bar.

Tanner met John Riggs in front of Pruitt's Dry Goods. For almost the first time he could remember, the doctor had given in to
Kansas heat to the point of taking off his coat; he carried it over
one spare arm, his sleeves turned back over his wrists and the
white shirt showing circles of sweat under the arms. "Well," he
said dryly, as he mopped his face with a pocket handkerchief,
"we've had the oratory and we've got our railroad. Now it's up to
us to prove whether we've got a town!"

Clark Tanner nodded absently. For some reason his thoughts
were still with the woman at the hotel, and it made him say without preliminary, "John, you've knocked around some. Did you
ever come across a man named Converse—a professional gambler?"

Riggs gave him a look. "I don't know what circles you think I run in, but if I have dealings with that kind it has to be in line of business. I've patched up my share of gaming-table casualties; Converse is not a name I remember. Why do you ask?"

"Something that came up," Tanner said, and went on to tell, briefly, about the woman and her questions. "I couldn't help but feel sorry for her," he said. "And admire her spunk to come so far by herself, looking for this missing husband. But I could only tell her there wasn't any town here last October, so there's no one could give her any leads."

The handkerchief in Riggs's hand went still; he peered searchingly at the other man. "Well, now—wait! October? I remember Beason saying he and Colby were on the ground about that time, laying out the town. True, they never filed their plat until later; but they were around, all right. And if the woman's husband actually made it this far, there's a chance one or the other might have seen him. You could ask."

Tanner shrugged. "Seems altogether too long a shot. It's my guess the man is lying dead by the trail, somewhere down in the Nations."

"Wouldn't cost anything to ask."

"If I can find them, in this crowd. I don't suppose either of them would be at the office." Nevertheless he started that way; Riggs for no clear reason fell in beside him, rolling down his sleeves and shrugging into his coat as they pushed a way through the mob.

When they passed Cotton's saloon a hubbub of male voices, loosened by drink, came from there. Someone shouted a curse, and there was a woman's muffled scream. The doctor listened with a grimace and a shake of the head. "You hear that? It has me a little scared. That's just a hint of what we can expect, if plans for this town even halfway work out. Damn it, we waited too long! We had all the warning in the world—and we're not ready!

"I have to admit," he added—a shade petulantly, Tanner thought, "I'm a little disappointed in Phil. We made him mayor, and we gave him the go-ahead and a free hand; and yet we're no nearer than we were to being able to cope with the trouble we know is coming."

It seemed a measure of the doctor's uneasiness that he would come out with open criticism of his best friend in this town. "You can't blame Phil," Tanner pointed out in his defense. "A week is no time at all, finding the man to wear a peace officer's badge— not unless you're willing to settle for a Morgan DuShane, or for some tough out of a barroom. Chances are, the man we want will have to be hired away from another job somewhere else for more money than he's already drawing. And that won't be done overnight."

John Riggs said glumly, "Especially when the council still doesn't have any money!"

"*He* doesn't have to know that. We can hope it's a detail we'll have ironed out before time comes to pay him!" Tanner added, "Phil spoke to me about a man named Jay Gerringer. Do you know him?"

"Gerringer?" Riggs pursed his lips. "Didn't he put down some trouble at Leavenworth, between the townspeople and some troops from the fort? Seems to me there was controversy about it."

"There's apt to be controversy," Tanner pointed out, "about any really capable man. But one who has the brains to stop trouble before it comes to a head should have a lot to recommend him. I told Phil we ought to find out the chances of meeting his price. . . . This place looks like it's still closed," he added, as they halted before the closed door of the town company office.

Riggs said, "I think I hear something." At the same moment Tanner noticed that the padlock was missing from its hasp. He put out a hand to try the door. His fingers had no more than touched it when he jerked them quickly back, startled by the sudden explosion of a gunshot just beyond the heavy panel.

For an instant he could only stand and stare foolishly at the grain of the wood, with the sound of the shot ringing in his head. John Riggs's startled exclamation broke him free of that. Remembering his own six-shooter, he fumbled it from under his coat as, with his free hand, he wrenched the knob and pushed the door open.

A sting of burned powder met him, and a swirl of black smoke that made him blink. A single, raking glance showed what there was to see: the Converse woman, her clothing awry and one glistening dark coil of hair loose from its pins, eyes staring in a face drained of color; and Nat Colby with his thick legs braced and his back against the railing that divided the office. There were bleeding tracks down one side of his face, where the woman's nails had raked it. Now a spot of red was beginning to spread high on his shirt front, near the right shoulder. His piggish eyes, dull with shock, stared as though in disbelief at the little nickel-plated gun leaking smoke in Rose Converse's hand. A sound of pain, like a whimper, broke from the big man's lips and, slowly, he began sliding down the partition, to a sprawling sit on the floor.

The muzzle of the gun slanted, following him down; Tanner, thinking the woman might take it in her head to shoot a second time, stepped quickly to place a hand on her wrist and deflect it. At his touch a long shudder ran through her, and she let him lift the weapon from her fingers. John Riggs, having taken matters in with a swift professional glance, went directly to the wounded man, but as he went down on a knee beside him he told Tanner, across a shoulder, "You'd better get her into a chair before she faints."

"I never faint," she protested, but she was shaking, and she gave no resistance as Clark Tanner got her through the gate in the railing and put her into the chair beside Nat Colby's own desk.

He had noticed the woman's reticule on the floor where it had fallen; he got it and laid it on the desk along with the gun, and then he went to look for water. There was a pail of it; he brought the dipper and held it while she drank, after which he said, "Mrs. Converse, can you tell us what happened?"

She spoke with an effort. "On his hand . . . my husband's ring. The star sapphire I gave Will myself. . . ."

Riggs lifted the hurt man's right hand, and the pale blue stone that Tanner had always considered out of place there gleamed in the dim light. The doctor commented, "He was sporting this the first time I met him, 'way last winter. I never saw him without it."

"You'll find initials inside the band," the woman said. Riggs slipped it off, with some difficulty; he had a look and, without a word, passed the ring across the railing to Clark Tanner. The engraved letters were plain enough: "W.C.–R.C." Tanner nodded and put the ring in the woman's palm, and her fingers closed on it tightly.

Riggs, meanwhile, was pulling back the hurt man's coat and

opening his shirt, to expose the bullet wound. Tanner asked, "How does it look?"

The doctor nodded. "A clean hole—too high to damage the lung. Didn't do the collarbone any good, but it should mend. See anything I can use to stop this bleeding?"

There had been a towel on a nail beside the water bucket; Tanner went and got it, and Riggs ripped off portions to wad into the two mouths of the wound and bind them in place. While he was thus occupied the door suddenly opened and Phil Steadman came in, accompanied by his redheaded nephew; apparently the report of that single gunshot had carried, because Tanner glimpsed curious faces before the door was shut again.

Riggs, looking around, nodded a curt greeting. "Phil, how about sending the boy to get my bag? He knows where I keep it— on a shelf just inside the door, where I can grab it quick." Barney Osgood hurried away for it, and once again the door was shut on the crowd outside.

"Now, what's going on?" Steadman demanded, and listened in unconcealed amazement to the hurried account he was given. He stared at the wounded man, propped against the railing, and then turned to Rose Converse. "Did someone suggest you ask at this office about your husband?"

"Yes," she told him, her voice still wooden from the shock she had undergone. "The man at the livery. At first there was no one here, but then he showed up and invited me in. And I saw the ring. . . ."

"How did he explain that?"

"He didn't. I expected him to lie—at least, to make up some story about buying it off a stranger."

John Riggs, wiping the blood from his hands, said dryly, "It takes brains to make a convincing liar. Nat Colby never had any."

"What did he tell you?" Tanner prompted.

"Nothing," the woman answered. "He just turned red in the face and began calling me names. He was so abusive finally that I got out the gun and told him I was going to turn him over to the authorities. That's when he tried to take the gun away from me, and—I had to use it!"

"I'd say you used it well," Steadman commented. "Let me see the ring a minute," he added. He checked the initials to confirm them; then, going over to Nat Colby, he went down on his heels. "All right, Nat," he said, speaking distinctly to penetrate the dazed fog that dulled the man's eyes. "You aren't too bad hurt to answer some questions."

When the eyes focused briefly, then slid away again, Steadman came near to losing his temper. "Will you look at me?" A hand shot out, seized Colby by the hair and pinned his head against the railing. The other hand held the ring within inches of his face. "I want to know how you got this," Steadman said roughly.

Colby looked at the ring, apparently without even seeing it. But then he *did* see it, and his reaction was violent—a contortion of his whole face, a feeble, scrambling attempt to push himself away and climb up the railing partition to his feet. Pain unmanned him. He collapsed, moaning; and Steadman, without mercy, bore in on him. "Start talking!" he ordered.

Despite the numbing agony of his chest wound, Nat Colby tried defiance now. Through tight lips he muttered, "I don't have to say anything to you!"

"By God, you'll say it to a judge!" Phil Steadman laid it out for him, not mincing words: "A man is missing. You have valuable property that belongs to him. Unless you have a damned good explanation and proof to back it, there isn't a grand jury that wouldn't indict you for murder!"

"Even *you* have got brains enough to understand that," John Riggs put in.

Apparently he had, because already they could see the weak defiance beginning to drain out of him. Scowling but uncertain now, as he sat on the floor clutching at his hurt shoulder, Nat Colby let his glance shift from Riggs to Steadman to Clark Tanner. "Quit staring at me!" he cried out suddenly, hoarsely. "I never murdered anybody. . . ."

They merely waited, and as the silence drew out they saw the fear begin. "I never!" Colby insisted, panic in his voice and in the loose shape of his mouth. "*It was Virg!*" Suddenly he couldn't get the words tumbling out fast enough. "I tell you, it was Virgil Beason. I *seen* him! He wouldn't listen to me. He—he finished him off and I watched him strip the money belt off his body."

Clark Tanner stepped to the desk where he had placed the

woman's reticule; he got the photograph and brought it back, to thrust it in front of Colby. "Was this the man?"

They saw the answer in his face before he nodded vigorously. "Yeah—that's him! That's the one. . . ."

"And what happened then?" Steadman demanded.

"Virg dumped him in a gully and caved the bank in on him. I can show you," Nat promised, babbling now, the sweat pouring down his cheeks. "I can take you to the very place. . . ."

For a moment no one could speak.

Tanner looked at the others, trying to judge if they were as appalled, as angry, yet actually as little surprised as himself. "What do you think?" he demanded.

"That he's still a rotten liar," John Riggs answered. "He's trying to put the whole thing on Beason—but he was in it too, up to his ears. He's every bit as guilty as his cousin. Having the ring proves it."

And Phil Steadman added, "I guess we know where at least part of the money came from, that they've been pumping into this town." He turned to the woman, then; her face white as bone, she had risen from her chair and was standing by the desk, with one hand on it and the other pressed to her bosom. He gentled his voice as he told her, "Ma'am, it looks as though there can't be much doubt. I'm sorry! Once this man has helped us recover your husband's body, I'm afraid there's nothing left to be done."

"There's one thing left," Tanner corrected him.

At the tone of his voice the others turned quickly. Steadman asked, "What do you mean?"

"I mean Beason! Whatever else, Colby has definitely hung the sign on him; and so he's got to be taken and bound over for a court hearing. There's no escaping it."

Riggs nodded slowly; he looked suddenly worried. "You're right, of course. But Virgil Beason's a different proposition from his cousin—smarter, and slicker; and if we're to credit Colby's story, then he's killed at least once already. He may not be taken easily. This is his town, for God's sake! And there's that Morgan DuShane he's been so thick with lately. I've heard report DuShane's a full-fledged gunman. What if he decides to deal himself in?"

Phil Steadman looked at the doctor during a silent moment,

that was broken only by the muffled sounds from the street outside. "If you weren't my friend, John," he said finally, "I'd think you were trying to scare me."

Abruptly he turned away, passed through the gate in the divider rail, and started pulling open desk drawers and slamming them again. Clark Tanner asked, "What are you looking for?" but got no answer.

Whatever it was he apparently failed to find it. He straightened for a thoughtful look about the office and discovered a wooden cabinet; he went to it, opened its doors, and with a grunt of satisfaction brought out an ugly, short-snouted weapon—a double-barreled shotgun. "I figured they must keep some kind of a gun around here," Tanner heard him comment, as he checked the loads. Apparently satisfied, he snapped the twin tubes into place again.

His friend Riggs observed him anxiously. "You know anything about handling one of those?"

"I know as much as I need. All you have to do is point it and pull the trigger, and the gun does the rest."

"Provided the other fellow gives you the time!"

Steadman shrugged and hefted the weapon, getting the weight of it. But as he started for the partition gate, Rose Converse was there with a troubled protest: "Please! I don't like anyone risking his life over this. I've had the answer to my question. And there's no way to bring my husband back."

He met her look soberly. "Believe me, Mrs. Converse—this goes beyond the matter of you and your husband. It's become a question of what kind of town we have here. We've got to prove that no man can get away with murder, not even if it's Virg Beason. And since we still have no law officer, as mayor of Eden Grove I'd say the job was up to me."

He gave a parting glance to the motionless hulk of Nat Colby, sitting in his own blood on the floor. "Doesn't look as though he'd be going anywhere," he told John Riggs. "But make sure he doesn't—use the lady's popgun if you have to. We'll worry later about what to do with prisoners, having no jail."

Riggs nodded, the mild eyes behind his spectacles showing their concern. "Watch yourself with Beason," he said anxiously. "And if DuShane's with him—for God's sake, watch them both!"

"I mean to."

Phil Steadman's manner, as he turned to the door, failed to hide the tension he was under. And seeing that, Clark Tanner felt a heavy kind of resignation settle in him. It was the last thing he wanted to do, but these men were his friends and suddenly he knew he had no choice. His hand shook a little as he brought the gun from under his coat; his voice was steady enough.

"Wait up," he told Steadman. "I'm coming with you."

# CHAPTER XVI

With the door of the office shut behind them, Steadman gave his companion a hard look. "Are you really sure about this?"

Tanner hesitated. He was certain neither Steadman nor John Riggs knew the truth about the injured hip that crippled him; he had never volunteered it, and his friends had chosen not to ask. For an instant he felt the urge to lay it out, as a warning of what to expect from Morgan DuShane; but he bit the impulse back. He didn't want his decision to sound like a personal vendetta against an old enemy, or on the other hand reveal how frightened he was at the thought of facing him again. So he shrugged and turned the question aside, saying only, "It's partly my fault you're mayor. The least I can do is back your play, if I can."

"All right. . . . It couldn't come at a worse time," Steadman added grimly. "Today of all days! But I guess no day would be the right one for something that can tear the town apart. We might as well get it over with."

"Where do we look?"

Shading his eyes, Steadman peered across the smear of sun and dust that was Railroad Avenue. The excitement of the official ceremony was ended. Bunting hung limp from building fronts, in the windless noontime; the speakers' stand was deserted, the band silenced and dispersed—likely, to the bar at Cotton's. Some part of the crowd remained, clustered at the station platform where the engine and cars stood motionless. "I guess that's the place to start," Phil Steadman said. "Last I saw of Beason, he and DuShane were headed there."

"Whatever you say."

At that instant they were hailed by Barney Osgood, returning with the bag he had been sent to fetch from Riggs's office. The redhead was staring at the shotgun and at Tanner's revolver. He would have moved to join them, but his uncle sternly waved him back. "Stay where you are. Give John a hand if he needs it."

"But—"

"You mind, now!" Leaving the young fellow gaping after them, they cut directly toward the depot, across the wide strip of yellow dust.

Still some yards distant from the cluster of people at the tracks, Clark Tanner told his companion, "I don't think they're here."

"I don't either." Steadman waved a signal to someone who was just leaving the place and the man veered toward them; he asked, "Have you seen Virgil Beason?"

Ogling the guns, the man told them, "Yeah, just now—him and that fellow DuShane. I had an idea they were going over to take a look at that casino, or whatever it is DuShane's putting up. . . . Hey—is something wrong?" He got no answer. An exchange of looks, and Tanner and Steadman had abruptly altered their course.

Cinders crunched underfoot as they stepped between the shining rails; then the casino was in front of them, a confusing forest of framing timbers and uprights. Tanner felt his hand sweating on the butt of the gun he carried pointing at the ground. He heard the click of the shotgun's hammers being thumbed to full cock. Steadman, he saw, had the twin barrels braced carelessly over his left arm; but his right hand was on the trigger housing and the knuckles showed white beneath the skin.

Virgil Beason came into view. And DuShane was with him.

Apparently they had just made a tour around the perimeter of the unfinished building; now, DuShane had paused to inspect something and Beason, seeing Tanner and Steadman, came on alone. He didn't miss the weapons. His frown showed surprise and a sudden caution as he halted, at a little distance, and called to them: "You looking for me?"

"That's right," Steadman answered. He held up where he was, waiting, and Tanner saw his strategy—he intended giving Beason a chance to come closer, separating himself from his companion. And Beason did, approaching a half-dozen steps before he stopped again. As he put his questioning glance on Steadman, his narrow features held a contained and crafty wariness. He would have been a fool not to know something unusual was afoot.

"Well?"

"There's trouble at your office," Steadman told him. "Some personal business," he added when the other made no move.

It was a good effort, but it didn't work. Beason might not have guessed that the idea was to get him alone, yet for whatever reason he apparently was not going to be budged any farther from where he stood. And now Morgan DuShane was coming up to join them, plainly curious to learn what was going on.

"What kind of business?" Beason demanded.

Phil Steadman drew a breath, evidently knowing there was going to be no easy way to do this.

"All right," he said. "It has to do with Will Converse. . . ."

The name plainly meant nothing to DuShane. He was eyeing Clark Tanner and the drawn gun, while Tanner tried to meet the look without revealing any hint of the pounding in his chest, the dryness in his mouth and throat. Beason, for his part, seemed a master at keeping secrets behind that narrow fox face of his. There was not the least flicker of emotion in him as he prodded his informer with a curt, "Go on. I'm listening!"

And Phil Steadman let him have it all: "Converse's widow is here. She identified the ring your cousin took from his body. And Nat Colby confessed to the whole thing—and named you the killer."

For a moment longer, there was still no reaction. Then Beason's mouth twisted and he dropped his arms and let out his breath in a slow, whispered, "Jesus!" He shook his head. "I knew that ring was dynamite," he went on in a tone that no longer held any trace of pretense. "I wanted to bury it with him; but Nat, like a fool—"

"Fool or not, he's charged you with murder."

"Oh, he would! No mention, I suppose, that it was him lost his head and started the shooting. He put the first bullet into Converse—I had no choice but to finish what he'd botched."

"Makes no difference. In the eyes of the law, you're equally guilty. And we've come to put you under arrest."

Morgan DuShane asked, "Do you think there's enough of you?"

The low-voiced question was a challenge; it struck across taut-ened nerves and brought him their full attention—and that was nearly fatal, because it gave Virgil Beason his opportunity. There was no sign, no change of expression; suddenly, and without warning, from somewhere in his clothing a gun had appeared in his hand and he fired it, point blank, at Phil Steadman.

A bullet of that caliber might have been expected to sweep him off his feet. He staggered though he stayed erect; but then, horrified, Tanner saw his friend start to double forward. Steadman's hand crimped the triggers of the shotgun and both barrels went off, straight into the ground at his feet, its double charge smashing the noontime stillness and blasting out a crater; he toppled and dropped prone across it. And through a ballooning of dust and powder smoke, Clark Tanner saw the face of the one who had shot him, and something in the deliberate manner of it stung him all at once to white fury.

Tanner had never pulled the trigger on a man before; almost without conscious direction his arm came up and the muscles of his hand and wrist worked convulsively. At that distance, he could not have missed. He fired twice, catching the strong jolt of the discharge against his palm; he saw Virgil Beason's face lose its shape, and then the man was twisting limply as he fell.

Often, Clark Tanner had wondered how it would feel to kill a man—he had expected at least a sense of remorse and shock. But for the moment, seeing Beason go down didn't even blunt the driving edge of his fury. He was already swinging the barrel of the smoking gun, until the figure of Morgan DuShane loomed above the sights. He was hardly aware of Beason's sprawled shape between them, or of Phil Steadman moaning and clutching a bleeding arm. "What about it, DuShane?" he challenged, in the confused echoes of the shooting. "You want a part in this?"

He had never expected to see loss of control, even blank astonishment, reflected in the face that had become the center of his nightmares. Swept on by his own fury while Morgan DuShane seemed to hesitate, he raged, "Damn you, will you use that gun you've got under your coat? Look!" He lowered his arm so that his own weapon, still dribbling smoke, pointed at the ground. "Now will you draw? I'll give you time—that's a promise!" And he waited, every nerve taut and the breath hot in his throat; while, facing him, Morgan DuShane stood a little hunched, one hand half raised toward the opening of his coat front.

Unbelievably, then, DuShane shook his head and let the hand

drop—but Tanner was sure that, for an instant, those strange eyes had held a brief, incredible flash of real fear. He heard the man saying, "I'm no bodyguard for Virgil Beason! I told you once before, I came here to open a business, not to use my gun. I have no part in this—and nothing to do with you."

He turned abruptly, shouldered roughly past someone who stood in his way and was gone, vanishing into the crowd that had somehow collected. Tanner still could not realize it was over until he was jarred by the sudden weight of a hand pummeling his shoulder. Parley Newcome was shouting in his ear, incredulous and gleeful: "He backed down! He was scared and he walked away from it! By God, the look on you—it almost scared *me!*"

Clark Tanner turned his head and stared at the old printer, only half comprehending. And then John Riggs was there with his bag, shoving to clear a space around Phil Steadman as he exclaimed, "Get away—damn it. Give this man room!"

Steadman had pushed himself to a sitting position, but his left arm was bleeding freely; as the doctor knelt and set to work, Tanner was stirred out of his shock to ask, "Do you think he's going to be all right?"

Steadman answered him, in a tight voice. "It hurts, but it won't kill me. Beason fooled me completely. Somehow it never occurred to me he had a gun, or that he'd start shooting. I was watching the other one. . . ."

Tanner's dazed glance moved on to the grotesque sprawl of the one he had shot. "Is he dead?"

"Beason?" The doctor nodded briskly. "Dead enough—I can tell without even looking close." He paused in what he was doing, to speak impatiently to the witless, staring onlookers: "For God's sake, try to do something useful!" He pointed at the dead man. "Get that thing out of the street. Pick it up and take it over to Booker's, some of you—It's his problem now. The rest—clear out while I get this man back on his feet!"

There was some reluctant shuffling of boots, but a good many of the onlookers showed no inclination to move on. Riggs, with an angry shrug, decided to ignore them and turned back to his work. He had Steadman's bloody sleeve cut away; his bag open beside him in the dust, he was doing a methodical job of swabbing the track Beason's lead had skewered in the muscle of the upper arm.

All at once, as his own head began to clear, Clark Tanner became aware of the gun he was still holding; with a sudden revulsion he thrust the weapon at Parley Newcome, saying harshly, "Take this, will you? I don't want to see the damn thing!"

"Why not?" his friend demanded bluntly, even as he accepted it. "Don't you realize you've done this place a favor, ridding it of a thing like Beason? Him and his partner! They called their town Eden Grove—but now we know it was built on murder!"

Riggs, unrolling bandages, had the troubled frown of a man trying to be fair. "Still, they did build it."

"And they meant to milk it dry!" Phil Steadman said through tight lips. "The town is going to be better off without them. Both of them!" he added. "There were plenty of witnesses heard Beason implicate Nat Colby in the Converse murder. He'll need smart lawyers, and every dime he can lay hands on, if he hopes to beat that charge!"

"So maybe here's our chance," the doctor suggested, nodding. "Pool our resources, and we should be able to buy out the partnership—at our price, likely. Give Eden Grove a fresh start."

"No more eight per cent interest, I hope!" Parley Newcome suggested dryly.

Clark Tanner had not really been listening to the talk. Suddenly he turned and started back across the street, alone; his hurt leg was bothering him again and Parley Newcome had no difficulty catching up with him as he was crossing the railroad ties.

Newcome still had the gun his friend had turned over to him. He said, as he stopped Tanner with a hand on his shoulder, "You don't act too happy about all of this. In fact you look pretty damn sour."

Tanner shrugged off the hand, saying gruffly, "I get moods. You know by now the best thing is to leave me alone."

"I don't think it's a mood," the other persisted. "You're still bothered about what happened just now. And I'd guess it's even more than that," he went on, in shrewd understanding. "You're thinking about the preacher girl. You're wondering if *she* watched it—or, what she's going to think of you when she hears."

H 22     Tanner turned on him. The excitement and near euphoria that had seized him during a moment of sudden rage was completely drained now, and in a kind of sick revulsion he cried, "Damn it, don't you realize I've *killed* a man? With her creed, and her up-bringing—she can't be anything but horrified!"

"You think so?" The older man seemed unmoved by the argument. "I figure she's tougher than that—and if she's not, this town is no place for her. There's two dead, now, for the cemetery up on the bluff; and either I'm no judge or that girl—and her brother too—have got sense enough to know we haven't even seen the start of the killing yet. I expect they'll know what you did today was no more than you had to."

"It's expecting a lot!" Clark Tanner grumbled.

"Everything's a gamble," Parley Newcome countered impatiently. He took his friend by the elbow then, turning him, with an ink-grimed finger pointed toward the sidewalk opposite. "There they both are. You showed you were no coward when you stood up to Morgan DuShane—now, prove it again: Go over and have it out with them. Give them the chance to show which of us is right!"

"No!" For the moment Clark Tanner, his nerve completely failing him, resisted the thrust of the hand that would propel him forward; but because knowing the worst was better than uncertainty, he resigned himself now to what he knew he must face sooner or later. "All right!" he said gruffly. "I'll go! Just quit shoving, damn it!"

And yet as he started across the sun-smitten dust, not bothering to disguise his limp, there was something in the look of that waiting pair—something, especially, in the hand Kit Lawless put out to him—that made him feel perhaps Parley Newcome was wiser than himself, and he had indeed only been fighting shadows.